Advent

of

Time

Hypocrisy & Reality

Book:3

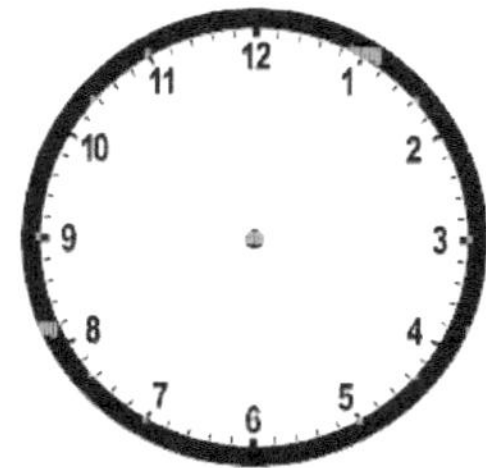 

fiction

by

'Videh' Arvind Kumar

1964 to 1967

(a novel)

(classes 3rd & 4th)

(*Maar-Haraa, Jhaajhar*)

Dedication

Advent of Time

(Hypocrisy & Reality:

Book 3)

Dedicated to my primary school teachers who propped me up as a tiny shoot to flourish as a towering tree!

Table of Contents

Dedication 2

Table of Contents 3

Copyright 4

Preface 5

Transcripts of *Hindee* letters and *maatraas* 5

1. 1964: The Advent Of Time 6

2. Determined To Remain Third Class: 9

3. Inoculation And Rustic Response 14

4. Innocence, Punishment & Psychic Pain 17

5. My Mother And Taaee *Fall Off The Ladder* 20

6. Cheeyaa *And Notion Of Getting* Riches 23

7. Poorab Pashchim..... *A Poet's Poetic Discovery* 25

8. Lathe Man & Chavannee (25 Paise) 28

9. Literacy And Breach Of Decency 30

10. Nayaa Daur *And My Adventurism* 35

11. Amongst The Elders: First Photograph. 39

12. Childish Theft And Paradise Lost 41

13. Realm Of Decimal Points 48

14. Hesitation & Lost Innovative Potential 52

15. Well Head, Spring and the Koel 54

16. First Feelings Of Romance 57

17. Language Teacher & Pronunciations 61

18. The Tongues Of The Unlettered ..63

19. Schooling Savagery 67

20. Human Society Is Not Different From Life In Wilderness 75

21. Hospitality Left To The Child's Mercy 78

22. The String Of Death 82

23. Father's Domain And Dharmashaalaa 85

24. The Vanquished Aspect Of Humanity 87

25. Callous Conventions 88

26. Neel Kothee *In The Wilderness* .90

27. Deprivations All The More 95

28. Baakhar *Bifurcated* 98

29. Father Ousted From The Town School 102

English Books by *'Videh'* 105

'विदेह' रचित हिंदी ग्रंथ 109

लेखक-परिचय 112

About the Author 113

Copyright

Advent of Time
(Hypocrisy & Reality:
Book 3)
First published in July, 2024
All rights reserved
@ *'Videh' Arvind Kumar*
Lucknow, India

Preface

'Advent of Time' is the third volume in the long fiction series entitled 'Hypocrisy & Reality' and covers the schooling period when the protagonist discovers the phenomenon of Time, and also, figuratively he feels that it's now his time, even as, he mysteriously discovers his latent potential and wisdom catapulting himself into the uppermost orbits of glory, fame and all round applause from his classmates, masters as well as teachers. To his own amazement as well as bewilderment! Nevertheless, this providential blessing is not without its blemishes in the shape of rancour and envy of fellow classmates and their patrons towards him. Even as, Nature never allows anybody pleasure and praise without at the same time associating with them the equivalent amount of pain and back-biting!

'Videh' Arvind Kumar
Aashrum, Lucknow, UP, India
July, 2024

Transcripts of *Hindee* letters and *maatraas*

Keeping in view the special pronunciations of *Sanskrit* words, and with a view to differentiating between the disparate pronunciations, we have followed the following regimen of transcription from *Devnaagaree* to Roman script. This clarification will help the readers appreciate the nuances of linguistic specificities and enjoy the text in truly desired sense. Moreover, the vernacular words, particularly nouns, have been italicized.

अ a, आ aa, इ i, ई ee, उ u, ऊ oo, ऋ ri, ए e, ऐ ai, ओ o, औ ऑ au, अं an, अ: :,
क ka, का kaa, कि ki, की kee, कु ku, कू koo, कृ kri, के ke, कै kai, को ko, कौ kau, कं kan, क: kah;

1. 1964: The Advent Of Time

Enter Protagonist

The ignoramus that I was, was there no more. The nut of 'one plus one' had been cracked. The knot of sums had been undone. The *'sim-sim'* of arithmetic had been discovered. I was the pole-star of the class now; not only class, but of the entire school! My teachers used to praise my exploits and feats to my father now and then. His affection – my father's -- for me had increased, of late. I used to sleep at *Gher* – the *Kheda*, the male residences -- with my father those days.

I can still recollect that my father asked me one day, "How many teachers are there in your school?" and I replied, "35 to 40." To which, my father explained, "Those are students, not teachers; teachers are those who teach you; you children do study, you are students." I felt gratified, although I had deliberately told him wrongly so that he could derive an amusing pleasure of educating a child, his son. I knew what he was asking, nonetheless, at times, it pleases to give others opportunity to preach us, by giving deliberately wrong answers.

In our neighbourhood, at the back of our male residences, there were residences of lower caste people, the so-called untouchables. They reared pigs, goats, hens, cocks etc for meeting their requirements of food; grains as they did not get enough, all having been grabbed by powerful upper caste people, like those of our family fold. The cock used to crow at the break of the day. My father explained to me that in olden days when there were no clocks or watches, the cock was the God's clock to wake up the human beings at the break of the day. I fancy, of late, the etymological similarity between the words 'clock' and 'cock' in keeping with their functions – of waking up people, sounding people about the aspects of time. And I marvelled at the Nature's spectacle and concern for its creatures, human beings included! And also, at the fact that one creature cared for the other one so much so as to wake him up in the morning! Lest it should keep sleeping forever! However, I was dismayed to think that the same cock used to be killed by the same human beings for eating, for their food, forgetting all the good the former might have done to the latter!

While I slept in the *Chaupaal* -- as we called the long hall we had at the *Khedaa* to our end -- I did also observe that I had the advantage of our grandpa's presence there; he shared his experiences, too, apart from telling us stories, multifarious life experiences, of which, he had plentiful.

Nonetheless, I also observed that at times there were ugly

quarrels and heated arguments between my father and my elder uncle, and I felt scared at those moments, since I had the childish notion that the squabble might culminate into fist fighting and violence and, in the process, the grown-ups would not care for a child's safety and sentiments. On the one side was my father who showed so much love for me, and on the other side, there used to be my grandfather and my elder uncle – *taujee* -- who were holding command of financial muscle of the household; I found myself in a dilemma – whom to side with, albeit I could do it only mentally. The bone of contention normally used to be concerning certain legal fights and suits that were being fought with our grandfather's counterpart – cousin -- and his issues. My father generally divulged the secrets and strategies of our side to the adversary while enjoying warmth of the bonfire available on their side in the season of winter, as was the practice those days, even as, people from village households in quite a large number assembled there daily, to chit-chat and gossip. I heard my father countering the grandfather and uncle duo by arguing that he could not tell a lie, and that the latter were indulged in secret stratagems against their adversaries. However, he was wrong. The suits were regarding the division of arable land,

the agricultural fields and it was quite natural that everybody would like to grab the best swathe, and also, nearer the village habitats. Even at my age I could discern the folly and foolishness of my father, and I felt myself siding with my grandfather and elder uncle if only psychically.

There were also the days when my father would be carrying me on his back to another side of the village where some saint might have come to give holy sermons to the villagers, or some singer might have come for giving a musical or singing concert, if you call it that way. Those were rustic songs – of valour, of patriotism, of chivalry and a pinch of romance, sort of cocktail. But that was a good pastime and ample entertainment for village folks who didn't have much of a job to do during winter season with all the sowing having been done, and nothing special having to be done as a daily chore, except the caring and rearing of domestic cattle, milch cattle *et al*. As of those days, I used to love my father and he used to love me a lot, too, I being his only son, possibly by that time. Piggyback riding his back, I felt safe and secure while traversing the rugged, dusty, swampy, puddled roads of the hamlet, moving as we did in the night time. Without any streak of light. In the countryside, immediately after Sunset it is called 'night' time. A little child like me might have tumbled over while walking on those paths – strewn with tiny boulders -- had I ventured to walk on foot on my own. I felt like flying in the air without facing the travails of land routes while lain on the back of my father. I, nonetheless, wondered why those industrious villagers did not take initiative to level the paths or alleys of the village; or why they did not make drainage for the passage of dirty water. Reason might be that they did not consider all those things as hazards or health hazards. In their daily lives they used to face much riskier prospects.

I had been studying in school, and daily our teacher would ask us to write something like numbers which he termed as 'date', import of which though we little could fathom. It was written somewhat like 12/10/1964. The first portion of the three-part number kept on changing daily; initially, we thought only first one-third kept on changing and it would continue till 100. However, it was not to be. After 30th the teacher asked us to again write 1 (one) in the first portion of the date. Now it became another puzzle concerning one! Does our teacher not know the numbers beyond 30? To add insult to injury, as though this much mystery was not enough, the Master asked us to change the second portion by one number additional, that is, by increasing the second portion of the date by one. At times, to add to our bewilderment, the teacher continued till 31 and we surmised that the teacher would have missed the deadline and would have recollected late by one day too much. Nevertheless, in our wildest dreams we could not think that the third portion of the wizardry that the function of 'date' was, would ever get modified; we rather assumed in our childish notions that the third portion was fixed, permanent and would never change; that it would ever remain 1964. 1964 was the year which was to remain constant as though! Everything else would undergo a change but the year would remain '1964' only.

There was no reason too for doubting our notion, nor was there any occasion to know otherwise; it was constant for months together in our consciousness since when we had started using the phenomenon of 'date'.

Nonetheless, on 31st of December that year, that is, 1964, it came as a bolt from the blue: all our notions of permanency of time as well as year got shattered. I was shouting 'Happy New Year! Tomorrow is Happy New Year!' imitating all others around, as though New Year heralded something entirely different from the current one!

"Which date would it be tomorrow?", asked my grandfather of me.

"It will be 1/1/1964!", I chimed sonorously, oblivious to the fact that I was in the wrong.

My *Baabaa* corrected me by saying that the next day would be 1/1/1965.

I was shocked to hear and discover it.

"But how come 1965? It was always 1964!", I enquired incredulously.

"The year will change from mid-night today and the next year naturally would be 1965. What comes next to 64?"

"Sixty five, no doubt, but does the year also undergo change in the 'date'?"

"Why not?", added *Baabaajee* with a look of utter surprise. His elder brother also expressed surprise at my foolish even as childish poser.

However, still in doubt, I ascertained from my playmates, "Would the year also change from tomorrow? Will it be 1965 from tomorrow?"

"Why, why not?", looked my friends quizzically in my face as though I were a duffer. I was a duffer numerically, mathematically once upon a time, not long ago; now I was eventually proving to be duffer temporally, as well.

"It means after one year it would be 1966 and so on!", I expressed my astonishment, to my elders' utter stupefaction. They were wondering about what was so abnormal about the change of a date that was troubling me so much! Nevertheless, it was abnormal for me indeed, and I was dumbfounded! To think of this ever changeability and eternal ephemerality of 'Time'!

Thus did take the 'Time' its birth on planet earth for me, the duffer! Thus far I was oblivious of the phenomenon of Time! For me everything was perennial so far. Now I came to realise that not only the human beings, but also, the time changes, seasons change, weathers change and landscapes change continually yet imperceptibly, without any commotion at all. It is only the living creatures, particularly, human beings, whose actions are done with lot of noise, hustle-bustle and tumult!

XXX

Table of Contents

2. Determined To Remain Third Class:

Enter Protagonist

Time had taken birth from the womb of my ignorance: the dates were changing every day, the months got changed every month – yet not all the months were equal as regards number of days, and the years were changing with every rotation of earth around its star, the

Sun! I had come to realise! How many more mysteries I had to explore yet? I wondered. How many myths had to explode yet? I marvelled at. I was a brilliant student in the eyes of my teachers and 'masters', as we called our teachers, and was relishing my glory to the full. The children who so far neglected me in all their errands now started taking notice of my existence. Many a head had rolled; those who were considered perennially on top of the mount of brilliance had been relegated to second or third rungs, however coupled with the concomitant rancour and malice having erupted against me, without any fault on my part; the only fault of mine being that I had become brilliant. Nonetheless, in this feat – my becoming brilliant – I had no say; I had become suddenly enlightened. I constantly was at a loss to know what my fault was that my classmates, especially, brilliant ones had started becoming jealous of me. Nonetheless, I was yet not admitted formally to the school's rolls.

Now as I had established myself, I thought I deserved a better treatment from my father, that he would admit me to school now. However, my father had other plans. He decided to admit me to school in 1965 when the session started. I was happy and gay that I would be in class fourth. But to my utter disappointment I was informed that I would be retained in class 3rd.

Despite being the most brilliant boy of the class? I ruminated. And I mourned the dropping of my one year. I complained to my mother: why should I waste my one year, but mother had no say in such matters. Father had decided in his wisdom to hold me back in class three only, during this session, as well.

Nonetheless, despite his being a cipher in mathematics, being a teacher and conscious of the implications of age in the light of job requirements in post-education period, he calculated the date of my birth so meticulously – although farcically – that my age at passing the Matriculation exam would in future fit exactly to what minimum was required for that purpose. That way I was benefited, no doubt. My father mentioned my date of birth as 1st of January, the New Year's Day, thereby reducing my age by almost one year and three quarters, and in turn, changing my Birthday. On thinking of this prospect, I felt sad instead of feeling glad as my real birthday fell on some other day while the people would wish me 'Happy Birthday' on an entirely different day. It was such a farce to be enacted for all the years ahead in my life! In my conviction there was no harm in retaining my actual date of birth intact as well.

Nevertheless, I have observed throughout my life that the teachers' fraternity resorts to such tricks so as to benefit their children. Whether this step was a benevolent one or unethical one, I am still uncertain and ambivalent about. But the dichotomy of my actual date of birth and the official date of birth always kept haunting me in my conscience. I had to live a falsehood throughout my life as regards my age. I could never celebrate my actual birthday! And I always felt awkward and guilty on my official birthday when people wished me!

When I complained to my father that he had advanced my date of birth putting me in trouble, he retorted, "You are merely a child knowing nothing; you do not know the implications of age. By this reduction in age, in future, you will not face the prospect of your age having expired for jobs." In hindsight now, I feel that my father was right. He acted being over obsessed with his son's welfare. And I never faced the prospects of age having expired. Still this is nothing short of a mystery that my age eventually expired for taking Civil Services Exam; but regarding that episode at some other as well as opportune time!

Thus, in the next session too I was studying in the same class, thereby giving me extra edge and sharpness in brilliance. Now I was an unrivalled champion of my class. The course of the class was already well-read for me; well-solved were all the sums of mathematics the previous year itself.

In our *Paathshaalaa* the singers singing patriotic or ethical songs used to come with the harmonium and they used to sing some song or tell some tale to the interest of us children. That was an interesting and entertaining thing those days. There were no such things as TV or mobile phones etc, not even radio was yet in vogue. Of course, there was one radio at our *Khedaa* – my grandfather's elder brother being a *Mukhiyaa* - the radio having been provided by the Govt. It was a wooden box inside which were fitted the valves thereby making its size quite large and unwieldy. From the box a cable – wire - was linked unto a distance of almost ten metres and the other end of this cable was dug inside the soil. In the pit where this other end was dug, water used to be poured; then only did the idiot box start uttering or gibbering something. When the radio box was in fine fettle it worked fine but mostly it worked as a jarring instrument, its voice was seldom audible or comprehensible for us children. In the evening, the worthies and wise people of the village assembled around the box to listen to the news or any drama being broadcast from there. It was like a magic box.

For us children, it was just like a small cabin of the speaker who was fancied to be sitting inside it and singing or speaking, the proof of which was that it required water intermittently to quench its thirst before speaking *a la* us human beings!

To the issue of incomprehensibility or non-grasping of the content being spoken on the radio by us kids, my grandfather clarified that in the beginning the ears, the hearing system, does not attune to the frequency of the speaker and after continuing to listen regularly, the ears start understanding and grasping and deciphering the code of language clearly. Also, that it takes some practice and adaptation! However, we were never adept at fathoming the spoken words on the radio.

Baabaajee also explained that the same thing happens when we listen to some other language or tongue. Initially, it sounds like gibbering of some idiot because we are not accustomed to the alphabet of that language. Later on, when we understand or learn the alphabet, we can clearly decipher what is being spoken, even if spoken at a very fast pace, that is, eloquently. In such matters my grandfather was a valuable asset for us. This facility others of my playmates or schoolmates did not have.

Those were the days of nascent country just having recovered from the yoke of foreign subjugation, still straddling and trying to stand on its own two legs. My grandfather used to say quite often, "It is a poor country; it has only been free hardly fifteen years or so. The nations take centuries to prosper and develop. Those countries which are advanced countries have prospered after two hundred years of their attaining independence. Have faith in the capability of our leaders."

Nonetheless, the disillusionment with the new dispensation had started setting in. The leaders had started showing their fangs. They had started filling their own selfish personal coffers with the public money. Those at the helms had begun promoting their sons and daughters in the corridors of power or in the administration. The bureaucracy had started creating a vicious cycle wherein only their children would be able to enter, no commoner could make it to civil services. Bribery had started taking the proportions of dragon's tentacles; sprouting it had started already immediately after changeover from British to the *Bhaarateeyas*, the Indians. ICS had virtually been converted into Indian Corruption Service; they were virtually the conduits for collecting ransom from the public for the wily and corrupt mafiosi called euphemistically 'politicians' or *'Netaajee'*; Provisions and food grains were not available and were rationed or released on permit. This 'quota-permit *Raaj'* had become notorious and obnoxious in the country and had become synonymous with 'political corruption'. And it was no more considered a shameful act -- the corruption; it was a norm during the time of the erstwhile regime!

However, my grandfather was not dismayed. He had seen the days of feudal lords, war lords and *Muslim* rulers and *nawaabs*. He often was heard commenting, "It was for the good of the country that Britishers overtook this country, else these *Muslims,* and even *Hindoo* rulers, would be only making the ladies become prostitutes and making prostitutes to dance on their dens, nothing else! Enjoying the sexual activity on the carnal body of the womenfolk at large had become the characteristic of the ruling class and feudal lords and *zamindaars* prior to the arrival of Britishers."

And I felt, that was true, however, the nationalists might object and protest!

But the euphoria of newfound term 'Freedom – *Aazaadee'* was still continuing. As I can recollect, probably the third Five Year Plan had been framed those days. My father had brought a large paper pamphlet whereupon the highlights of that development plan were printed. It was pasted on the *kutcha* wall of another brother of our grandfather who was the *Pradhaan* of the village at that time. For us little souls, that was a spectacle; the printed words. We gathered there and soon were hounded out contemptuously by the elder ones. They had little regard for the sentiments of the little souls; the elders. That was a typical vice of feudalistic people: they were insensitive to the sentiments of little children, women and down-trodden especially.

I can still recall one shattering memory wherein we children – civilized and polite ones – were assembled around the idiot box, the radio, and trying to make out what was being said. One of our ill-behaved elder uncles who was notorious throughout the area for his insolence and bestial temperament was also listening to the news there. However, children were children, they became restive and started bickering among themselves. Our elder uncle lost patience and rushed towards us children menacingly and used all sorts of foul and depraved language, including 'fucking' of our mothers and sisters. We got scared and ran away thinking ill of this seemingly adult person who was decidedly an insane or insensible one. We children seemed to be more sensible than this adult of the feudalistic fold was.

Whatever Plans would have been prepared by the then Govt, yet the progress on the ground was nowhere to be seen. A tradition had developed in the then set up to show the things on paper and grab the entire money to their own selfish pursuits, be they public leaders, be they Govt servants including bureaucrats, be they contractors; all were in cahoots and were skinning the public just like the Britishers might have done – even the latter did not do like these native leaders, the looters, to be precise. It seemed as though the then regime had won the 'Freedom' only for replacing the Britishers for looting the country. The former were siphoning off the money and country's resources to England and here were these new rulers, native rulers, who started siphoning off the money of the country to Swiss banks. Swiss bank accounts had become synonymous with leaders' accounts and the accounts for stashing away the black money of the corrupt.

And it was yet 1965 only! Hardly over 17 years had passed after transfer of rule from Britishers to select natives, the stooges of Britishers!

And I was in third class! Retained deliberately in third class by my supposedly wise father! Despite my being on top of the class! It seemed, alike my father, the country too had decided to retain its stature in third class only!

XXX
Table of Contents

.

3. *Inoculation And Rustic Response*

Enter Protagonist

The moment I am writing this, recently I have been inoculated for the dreaded disease of Covid-19. And this we – I and my wife – did get of our own volition and after lots of initiatives taken by us and hardships faced for getting it.

Nevertheless, there was a time during those initial school days when this inoculation used to be a dreaded word for us kids. In our village, at times, the medical workers, the medicos as we call them presently, of the Govt used to visit and persuade the parents to get their children inoculated, however, to little success. Most of the parents were childish in their demeanour like their children only, rather worse off mentally; they dreaded inoculation and vaccines more than they dreaded the potential risk of diseases, like, small pox, polio, measles etc. The fallouts of not getting their children vaccinated were pathetic, since the children of most of such foolhardy parents perished getting afflicted with fatal diseases, or were rendered handicapped by diseases like polio.

It was in the wake of newly acquired power -- the power to rule the country -- that the then prevailing Govt was taking various welfare measures for keeping the health of the populace sound. A sound bodied citizenry only can make a country worthy of respect and fit for living. Though lot of degeneration had set in following the natural and animal instincts of human species having raised their heads, of late, there were some people and officials who were still holding forte and doing their duties religiously: like, the medicos in our area. They seemed to be really interested in the welfare of us children, in our sound health, for they made it to our village facing all sorts of hardships of weather, climate, season and rusticity of populace, apart from facing the volley of protesting voices of rascals in the rural area.

Whenever, in our village, people saw the medicos come from the nearby village where PHC – Govt hospital, in simple terms -- was located, they fled to the fields and wilds to hide themselves as well as their wards so as to avoid the prospect of getting vaccinated. Children cried bitterly if vaccinated; sometimes they fell ill as well, as was natural, even as, it was considered to be a salutary effect of vaccination as per the medicos. Vaccination or discovery of vaccine,

that is, serum therapy, was the first discovery awarded the Nobel prize for Physiology or medicines in 1901 to a German scientist Emil Adolf von Behring. He had invented this therapy, specifically, against Diphtheria. Much water has flown since then down the Thames and Ganges, and vaccines for multiple diseases have been invented or prepared, and the scenario presently is that with the birth of a child these days the medical staff prepare a chart for vaccination or inoculation of the baby in near future, for which, the dates are pre-decided, for the sake of efficacy of vaccines and for the sake of healthy growth and development of the body and mind of the child. That's sensible and the salutary effect of the scientific developments made over the century gone by!

My father was an exception in that respect, however. He did not forbear taking of doses of vaccination for his children; may be owing to his coming regularly in contact with the medicos on the way while going to his school where the medical staff would also ply, heading towards their hospital or PHC, to be precise. He made us children offer ourselves to the medical staff, however, we cried. And cursed our father: 'All other fathers are so good as not to subject their children to such tyranny as inoculation, to that dreaded wheel which scratches the skin of the child's soft arm to inject the vaccine in the blood veins!' How at divergence the perceptions of parents and children may be! This is a fitting example of that phenomenon, that dichotomy between the perceptions and thinking of progeny and their parents. But somewhere in our hearts we felt that this painful exercise – sort of baptism with fire, with the scratching wheel – would be for our good, for our parents would not expose us to such pains without substantial gains to be got in return. And returns we did get in the form of not falling prey to those specific and dreaded diseases, like, small-pox – the *Maataa* as they called it, the measles – *Khasraa* as they called it. People so far during unscientific days thought, the disease was due to the wrath of *Sheetalaa Maataa* that resided in our garden which we adored so much on so many occasions, possibly exactly for this reason. The vaccine was the undoing of *Sheetalaa Maataa*! Presently, I see there is no *Sheetalaa Maataa* anymore there, even as, there is no garden anymore, the entire thing having been gobbled up by the greed and myopia of the progeny of those who had grown those gardens. People even in villages have since shed such illogical notions as regards inoculation, and have adopted the solid path of scientific

knowledge – the *Vedas* of medical science!

Sheetalaa Maataa, that is, small pox disfigured the face of the children by creating stains on the face or by destroying the eye etc. in case it inflicted its venom inside the eye. Even our aunt, the younger sister of my father, had a face full of poke marks created by small-pox in her childhood. There were many such people in our village and at other places, too. Polio is and was a still more dangerous scourge and many of our relatives had children who were incapacitated by the polio for life. Due to the ignorance of their parents, or by the polio? However ignorant one might be, one has to acquire essential knowledge for the requirements of living, lest one should pay very heavy price. Likewise, however, innocent and ingenuous one might be, one should acquire the wherewithal to live life oneself, and also, for one's family, like, food, shelter and clothing before jumping into the arena of marriage and procreation of issues unmindfully, lest one should pay very dearly in the manner of living the wretched life of penury throughout.

Unfortunately, just the opposite has been happening in society, in the world: people incapable of sustaining even their personal self consider themselves worthy of getting married and procreating children whose numbers they do not decide; they leave it to the intensity of their lust, to the creator of universe! Begetting children is their prerogative; however, arranging food, shelter and clothing is the responsibility of God – that unknown entity which is found nowhere – or of the Govt – which is indebted to such wretches by virtue of the latter's power to cast their votes in favour or against the Govt. Pathetic! Pathetic prospect is this voting system, which obliges the rulers to stoop low to any extent, and props up indolent and lustful people to beget dozens of children and leave them on to the streets and roads to beg unabashedly!

No question of their vaccination or education or culturalization! The result is that millions of animals, though in the shape of human beings, are seen stretching their palms before every passer-by whether in cars or trucks or on foot at the road-crossings in urban areas. At night, this unorganised army of seemingly human cattle is engaged in carnal pursuits and crimes without any qualms about ethics, morals, civility and culture *et al*. Poverty is not being created, it is being begotten through such crowds on roads, on pavements, in the slums and in the shanties! Poverty is getting birth in India at a very rapid pace. Unless it is checked, it is taken care of, through drastic measures, the country cannot expect freedom from the menace of vulgarity, crime and poverty in the years to come. These are not the days of medieval era when not infrequently some hordes of marauders whether they be from *Turkey*, or from *Mangoliaa*, or from *Afghaanistaan*, or from *Persiaa, et al* would venture to plunder and slaughter the masses of the land, and all such superfluous masses would

be wiped off. Or, if not the looters, even the local fiefdoms would consume them in the internecine wars amongst themselves, keeping themselves at safe distance from such fights personally, and letting fools murder and get murdered, without any cause!

XXX

Table of Contents

1.   *Innocence, Punishment & Psychic Pain*

Enter Protagonist

I had become the crown prince of my school and had now no fear of any downfall or humiliation at the hands of either teachers or the fellow students. *Chiranjee* had started reconciling, too, with me, and also, with the fact that it was none of my fault if I had become suddenly a brilliant prodigy of the school. Now it was up to *Chiranjee* himself to beat me in competition, that is, studies.

Nonetheless, during this process, I had developed a notion in my mind that being a brilliant student and a disciplined student and a proclaimed polite and gentle chap of the school I was not liable to any reprimand, rebuke or punishment by my teachers. Notion is notion, another person may or may not be harbouring the similar notions in his mind!

One day it so happened that during the salubrious season of winter, our class was not being taken by any teacher, may be due to some teacher being on leave and the available teachers taking senior classes. We were, therefore, made to sit aside at a platform where ample amount of sunshine was yet present. It was however the afternoon session, just prior to the time of leaving the school. An empty mind attracts *Shaitaan* to roost upon it: the children were not able to cope with the lack of any errand or sensible job. It's not easy to kill the time without any work. If there is no task at hand to keep the mind busy with, the time eventually kills the living creature. That's why death is also called *Kaal* – literally, the Time. The children started bickering amongst themselves which eventually developed into a ruckus and loud noise ultimately. They started making all sorts of mischiefs. I was sitting amidst them – the naughty figures - content in my conviction that whatever might be the misdeeds and mischiefs of my colleagues amidst which I was sitting, no punishment would be meted out to me by the teacher, for I was an acknowledged gentle boy; I knew it very well and was proud of this appellation for me used by everybody who knew me including the teachers.

The ruckus continued for some time until the patience of the teacher teaching another group at the nearby spot of sunshine gave way. He once warned the kids, but to no effect. Ultimately, he came rushing with a stick in his hand and raising the same up threatened the students that he would beat and flog everybody. But he did not beat anybody: he was a known soft-hearted soul as the children knew very well. Nevertheless, he commanded everybody to take the posture of a cock –'*Murgaa Bano!*'

At his command all the children assumed the posture of a cock by picking their ears with hands tucked from inside their legs and bending their backs, with head earthward. And the children did it gleefully, without any sense of remorse or repentance or guilt as if they had got what they were wishing for since long. Still as cocks, they were busy making mischiefs amongst themselves. I thought I would be exempt from the group punishment; however, the teacher unmindfully rebuked me why I did not assume the punishment posture – the cock posture. I could not gather courage to clarify my stand that I was not guilty, that I was not making any mischief, that I was sitting silently, that he himself could vouch that I was a good, gentle chap. I too assumed the cock posture however mournfully, unlike all other playmates, classmates. At this apparent injustice on the part of the teacher done to me without discriminating among the wrong-doers and the innocent ones engendered a sense of revengeful ill-will towards the teacher in my heart. What sort of a world and society it is where they command punishment *en block* without caring for the sentiments of innocent children or people. That was a shocking incident in my life – first ever taste of societal injustice outside my household.

At this sense of victimisation without any cause or fault on my part, I started feeling like weeping and ultimately I broke down. I started sobbing silently and tears started flowing from my eyes. However, I was trying to suppress my voice so that fellow boys did not come to know that I was weeping and shedding tears. Yet, the nearby boys quite smart as they were and every child is, immediately got the wind of my state of predicament. Instead of showing any sympathy towards my condition, some of them started commenting mirthfully, *"Murgaa kukudkoo kar rahaa hai!"* (The cock is crowing: *cock-a-doodle-doo!*); and hearing this, some others started laughing, to add insult to my injury. I would not be having that level of sense of humour at that time inasmuch as I felt pained at this treatment on the part of my class-fellows. However, this mirthful remark by the boy of my age, in the similar condition of misery, compelled me to have second thoughts about my approach to this *en mass* punishment.

I may not have been the only person who was not guilty of any wrong doing, many others also like me would have been there in the class; they were taking the punishment gleefully and participating in the merry-making at my cost in the wake of this remark. The sense of special privilege for myself had been created in my childish heart and this was the first incident that exploded the myth.

I could now realise that notwithstanding one's actions if one's company is bad and suspect, and if one keeps company with criminal-minded and corrupt persons, there is no way one should be spared. The human beings do not strain their brains to discriminate between innocent and guilty! It's not British criminal law that holds that 'no innocent person should be punished, let dozens be let off notwithstanding'; it's the natives' law of the land, of *Bhaaratmaataa*!

The unjust punishment continued for its full length and I felt tired inasmuch as this was my first baptism with fire – with such physical punishment -- in the wilderness of literacy. It signified the law of the jungle, figuratively put.

After the punishment period was over, I felt ashamed to have been doubly punished – first by having to take the cock posture unjustly, then by the sarcastic remark by my class-fellows utterly insensitively. The latter conveyed the episode of my sobbing to the teacher, at which he laughed, too. For him, such things were trifling and not worth taking cognizance of. In the jungle, most of the harms are done to innocent and gentle animals only by those endowed with brutish power. For me, of course, it was a life-changing episode. Some of my friends also showed sympathy towards me saying that I was innocent and the teacher ought to have spared me. But who cared!

I set off musing that there was no way out of such situations: I could not sequester myself from the midst of that naughty lot sitting as we were in a congested spot and were bound to sit together. Still today, I have not been able to solve that knotty issue of undeserved punishment meted out to me notwithstanding my acknowledged innocence.

Throughout the way to my home I kept on contemplating of my unjust punishment and humiliation: despite my being a good-demeanoured boy, taking all sorts of precautions not to do anything untoward. What sort of a world or wilderness is this? At home I told the entire sordid story to my mother, my sole preserve, and emptied my heart's angst against the teacher and the school. At the mention of '*Murgaa Kukudkoo kar rahaa hai*', my mother could not help smiling and I too smiled now when there was no risk of repetition of the punishment, and also, that the incident had gained some distance in time. Time thus transforms the countenance of events and changes its colours and effects. Even the most gory and tortuous of incidents that might have happened in the past become relishable tales when told at leisure time and in the state of relative comfort and peace in future. The same incident! The effect of passage of time! An illusion! A hypocrisy!

XXX

Table of Contents

5. *My Mother And* Taaee *Fall Of The Ladder*

Enter Protagonist

In the bigger *Baakhar*, actually, our portion was merely a

small corner, to be true; of which, merely half room was for our use. Not even half the room, a lengthy room as it was, we were actually in the middle of the room and on the other side there was our elder grandmother's occupancy: *Badee Amma's* establishment, if one would like to call it.

One may gather the impression as to what sort of a clumsy and cloistered arrangement it was; but people were accustomed to such bizarre situations of living in the feudal environs; there used to be no privacy at all, there was no closet to keep the valuable things in: at the most the valuable things would be kept dug in the soil, in the soil, in the floor somewhere. Mother Earth was the only reservoir for safe-keeping of our valuables, if at all we possessed any!

Since the habitats were *kutcha* though sturdy and durable, they needed regular repairs and white-washing and smearing with cow-dung paste. And these chores were taken up after the monsoon season was supposed certainly to have left the sky and our geographical area.

On one such a day when I returned from the school, I found to my bewilderment and sorrow that both my mother and my elder aunt were lying in the beds, bed-ridden, so to say. It was an ill omen! For me, the child! How should I get food

and who would take care of me, the child, a school going one? Who was dependent for every small chore of daily living on one's mother! Who would prepare me for school now onward? I set off ruminating on a chain of musings in my mind and heart.

We had one of our aunts unmarried by that time there only, unmarried yet: she was the younger sister of my father. She came to my rescue even though she was living with our elder aunt, *Taaee*, and I had the notion by this logic that she would not do me any favour for she did not get any favour from our father. The reality was not that awful however; despite our cooking separately, the blood bonds still worked, not defunct yet. I was told that my mother and elder aunt, instead of engaging some artisan for white-washing the habitats, had taken upon themselves the task of doing the job themselves. Without taking their male partners into confidence somehow. They intended saving money which was so scarce. Now when they had fallen and there was no way to hide their hurts: the arm bone of my elder aunt – *Taaee* - had been broken, that could not be hidden anyway. They were using ladder, and the small ladder slipped and both the good ladies acting as they were as labourers and artisans came crashing down hurting themselves and breaking their bones and bruising their bodies here and there.

Their intentions were good, yet they got hurt; what was wrong with the Nature's law? I set off musing when I heard about this mishap. More than the hurt, there was the fear of rebuke and reprimand by their husbands when the latter would return in the evening from their respective schools. More so, the husband of my mother – my father; he was a perfectly senseless creature! I started worrying about the evening scenario as to what it would be. I could easily envisage and predict the dreadful scenario that would take place in the evening at my residence whatever it was. It was so mathematically predictable, my father's misdemeanour as well as irascibility! As though his histrionics were to be as an icing on the cake: flogging on top of the bruises of my mother!

I approached my wounded mother gloomily and enquired of her state of hurt, and found her to be in good humour as against my apprehension that she would be immobile due to hurt and broken bones. Amazingly and humorously, she apprised me that she did only feign to have broken her bone, and as if feeling excruciating pain, simply so that her elder partner – my *Taaee* -- did not feel envious that only she alone got hurt in the enterprise, the misadventure. I was pleasantly surprised and felt relieved to think that at least my care would be taken as regards the provision of food and preparation for going to school. Selfishness is such an overpowering attribute that entire Creation is governed by it preponderantly.

In the evening, when my father and elder uncle returned from their respective schools, they felt sorry and said only two words of chastisement to their ladies that instead of saving paltry sums of money they had intended, they had eventually ended up creating the circumstances whereby more money was to be expended on treatment of hurts and wounds, apart from the loss of man-days which could have been utilised for doing some other creative domestic chores.

Surprisingly for me and all the rest, my father also did not create any fuss!

In this behalf, I recollect a story told to us by our grandfather during our evening sittings. He ended the story by quoting a couplet:

'Sikhvee sikhav kare to saaje,
Nahin to laath mongro baaje!'

(meaning thereby, if a skilled person performs a technical job that's alright, but if an ignoramus and unskilled person performs the same technical job, he gets battering and gets wounded in the process.)

My mother and elder aunt did not know the job how to whitewash and repair the habitat and could not assess the risk associated with climbing a ladder; and they simply considered the notional saving in whitewashing by doing the job themselves, with the result that instead of savings they ended up incurring much more expenses apart from loss of man-days for domestic labour, thereby disrupting the normal routine of both the households.

My mother, in fact, recovered soon as she was not hurt firstly; she was simply feigning to have been hurt. How crazy is the human world, human society! One rues other's not getting hurt more than one's own getting hurt!

XXX

Table of Contents

0. Cheeyaa And Notion Of Getting Riches

Enter Protagonist

Beside our village we, that is, our grandfather possessed large tracts of arable land. And having land in and around the village itself was not an easy task; it took lot of clout and connections in higher echelons of administration and Govt. And our grandfather had those connections, by virtue of his schooling at *B R College, Aagaraa,* where he had made friends with who's who of the *zamindaars* and *taallukdaars;* and when the latter attained higher authorities in the Govt, administration and judiciary etc. they did not forget my grandfather although the latter did not go for any job whatsoever. Otherwise too, he and his now late cousin had both plucked in the Matriculation exam of British era and had dropped the idea of pursuing anything further in the arena of education, studies or literacy, whatever one might call it.

Though not prone to such tendencies as recommending to his friends for some favours, merely his being associated with the higher authorities and the knowledge thereof percolating down among the lower officials facilitated favours for my grandfather without having to ask for. Thus, even in the law suits that he fought with his siblings, he won the cases and the result was that we had large swathes of land in the vicinity of the village, virtually at stone's throw from our male and female residences, *Khedaa* and *Baakhar,* respectively.

Around one such field our elder uncle – *Taaujee* – had drawn a boundary, head high. In that field, our aunt, his wife, had strewn the seeds of castor which sprouted before our eyes, grew, spread their broad fronds like the wings of vultures and became trees spreading their shaded canopies overhead, all before our eyes! All that before our eyes! Like a miracle, the vacant land, that is, the field got converted into a green garden; and it offered such a spectacle indeed to our eyes – yes of the kids! For us children! We played and marvelled at the Nature's bounty and magic with which it converts the inert and empty soil into such magnificent vegetation as this one. The unseemly view of the dry land inside the bounded area at one time, became a green garden for us children, for our daily merry-making. The trees of the castor, though having soft branches, were of low height and we kids could clamber upon them quite easily.

And before our eyes only, yet another miracle took place: the trees bore flowers, followed by buds, and then fruits of castor, which were marvellous for us children, very soft too, easy to crack, and also, some of them cracked on their own when ripened. This crop of castor produced a large amount of castor seeds and huge stock of fuel wood for our aunt, our *Taaee*. In the process, I somehow developed a crazy notion that from a fistful of castor seeds the owner had earned a huge amount of produce, in return, and in turn a huge amount of money, simply by applying one's brain power, that is, strewing merely a fistful of seeds in the soil. That's it! The rest of the job was done by the Nature itself automatically. To benefit from it, to get rich, of course,

the seed sower had to harvest the crop and arrange its judicious sale in the market. If one does not take steps even towards that much, nothing would happen, crop or no crop, harvest or no harvest. Nature does its own job but conscious beings are required to do their part too in the drama of life, so as to live a sensible and happy life, or to avoid wretchedness at the minimum!

This entire episode of castor seeds metamorphosing into a garden, and then producing huge harvest, and fetching sumptuous sale proceeds for our aunt and uncle, fascinated me like anything. Our father had no share in that produce and riches, however; and I felt deprived and depressed to think that the entire pleasant experience was of no monetary consequence for our own family, that is, my father's lot. In most of the affairs agrarian, this used to be the case; my father did not have any share in any such bounties. Why, I didn't know! Probably his lack of concern for such seemingly trifling things! Nonetheless, I have come to realise after living for all these years that neglect for such small stitches in time leads to huge leakages in one's fortunes in future requiring nine stiches ultimately. And it did happen practically in case of my father; he was converted into a super duper pauper in his heydays proper.

Thus this *Cheeyaa* (castor

seed) episode taught me a great deal in lessons in riches. In my childish discourses, of course, with my play-mates, I linked it specifically with *Cheeyaa*: that producing *Cheeyaa* led to riches. I also suggested to my mother for sowing *Cheeyaa* in our fields so that we could also become rich and could get rid of our lack of money which is also called poverty, but they – my parents -- did not heed. Both of them were jointly hell bent on becoming and remaining poor! And for good! I despite being a child of tender age was perturbed due to the abnormally straitened financial and food condition of my father's family. It seemed to me more owing to the foolhardiness and lack of sense on his part than owing to any lacunae or defect in the scheme of Nature or due to that phony phenomenon called ill fate or Providence. My father did not heed anything sensible, especially, if it concerned agriculture or Mother Nature.

I thought, our aunt would sow the seeds every year and we would enjoy the plays in the temporal castor garden, but even our aunt did not pursue this activity anymore despite it having turned out to be so lucrative to her, to my mind. The bounded area again became drab, dry and dusty. I wondered at the insensibility of elders of my extended household; they could not even enjoy the creation of a temporary garden created so easily by benevolent Mother Nature, whereas other orchards took decades to assume that much greenery, that much splendour!

I craved that crop of castor throughout my life in the vain hope that its harvest would remove our family's, our father's poverty, but nobody ever heeded my good counsel. Why they didn't and why I felt so intensely, I couldn't fathom that chasm, too!

XXX

Table of Contents

7.   Poorab   Pashchim.....   *A Poet's Poetic Discovery*

Enter Protagonist

Break-through I had got in my school and was well established as a prodigy with God-gifts of intelligence and brain-power; and I was myself surprised at this *Siddhi* of mine that I had attained without any special sacrifice or without having performed any strenuous penance. Simply a condemning remark by my father was the price paid for all this wonderment! I was so confident those days! I started considering myself special and all other fellow children as inferior mortals somewhere in my mind. The icing on the cake was in the shape of my father being a teacher in the town, and with a clout and name, more so, because of his so-called grand lineage – *uchch khaandaan,* as they dubbed this dubious phenomenon!. People were under awe of his pedigree. There was something indeed and amazingly spectacular about his pedigree as we have discussed hereinbefore. Nonetheless, pedigree was pedigree, and that had crossed its expiry date. We people were no more than mere commoners now, and that was the truth of the then prevailing times.

But alike my father, I too was under an illusion that I had a great pedigree, an *uchch khaandaan.* Not only this, I had few more feathers in my cap: my grandfather was the only personage in the area who knew English, and that was an unparalleled asset for us, having very high premium which none else could match in the entire area. Then, my father was the only personage in the area who was a graduate – the only graduate -- in the entire area around and this fact was intentionally popularised and made known to all and sundry. Meaning thereby, all the stars were in my favour! Only the money and riches was not there, nor was there ample food – even cereals -- to fill our bellies, and there was ever a sense of despondency permeating the household proper of my father. All around amongst his relatives there everything was resplendent, pleasant and well off. Even if money had been there, the attitude of my father and his lack of sensibility, and lack

of sense of impermanence about everything in the world, would have been cause enough to render the atmosphere suffocating and claustrophobic for us family members in any case. And it was so in our habitat: the dwelling unit proper of my father!

Yet, I was happy at school.

One day I was treading the way to my school all alone. On the way, when I reached near the *Neel Kothee,* an inspiration entered my mind that I was so brilliant that I might be able to compose poetry even. All great men of repute, who are immortal in fame, were poets or authors, I thought. My notion was like that only: the written word itself was such an awesome thing and the writer ought to be the only entity unsurpassable in greatness indeed in the whole creation!

I started musing and singing:

> *Jidhar saamne sooraj ugtaa,*
> *Udhar khade ho munh karke tum,*
> *Theek saamne poorab hotaa,*
> *Aur peeth peechhe Pashchim.*

(Meaning thereby, do stand erect facing the rising sun; in front of you there would be the East, on the rear would be the West, as simple as that. I mean, directions!)

It was purely common sense and in fact a narration of facts. And I got elated as if I had composed this poem myself out of some divine inspiration; as though I had become a great poet. Immediately, I came to realise that this was not a poetic inspiration, rather, I was chanting merely the rhyme that was there in my school text book. The subconscious mind has spectacular delusionary powers; whatever is accumulated inside through various sources, that only comes out in various forms, which we take as our own original product or composition and marvel at its weirdness. However, the prophets and sages of the old were humble enough to deny the knowledge that they imparted as their own, rather, they attributed the same to Almighty, some unknown source of intelligence and inspiration. Be it the *Holy Quraan*, be those the *Vedas*, be those the *Old* or *New Testaments* etc! Their purveyors never claimed that those were their own specific wisdom!

I recited the entire rhyme that was in my book and felt gay at yet another if only modest achievement that I had memorised the poem by dint of my common sense: I did not know by then that I could recite the poem by heart; it felt so tough when reading in the book at school. Here, on the way, in a merry and calm mood, when I associated it with the four directions, it became so easy to remember and I completed:

Baayeen or tumhaare uttar,
Daayeen or tumhaare dakkhin,
Chaar dishaayen hoteen hain ye:
Poorab, Pashchim, Uttar, Dakkhin!

(Meaning thereby; to the left of yours is the North and to the right is the South; this way, there are four directions, viz; East, West, North and South!)

Wallowing in the bliss of this new found realisation, the enlightenment, I reached school and disclosed this discovery to my friends and felt a sense of *déjà vu!* It was another *Eureka* after the earlier episode of legendary 'One plus One' problem! This filled me with the confidence that I could memorise the poems, as also, recite them so effortlessly. Reproducing anything as such is really a God gift! It is taken away in the advanced age, however, that's why I say that it is a great gift to have the capacity to recollect the things, events and the proper names of persons, places and other things; otherwise the life becomes unbearable and abominable, for oneself and for others, as well.

The feeling of directions filled me with the concept of Space. Time had already been invented on the New Year's eve that year, and now it was its sibling the Space, that caught up with me on the way to my school at a moment of merriment, placidity and calm, besides, of course, the dreaded proverbial *Neel Kothee*. The traditionally inculcated dread of *Neel Kothee* could not block my childish reverie on this equally childish discovery!

XXX

Table of Contents

8. Lathe Man & Chavannee (25 Paise)

Enter Protagonist

Bhaagadbhoot was our teacher those days. He was supposed to be very strict but a very effective teacher indeed he was. His personality was very impressive, even as, he was from the ancestry of *Jajaat (Yayaati)*. Although I had no difficulty with studies, nonetheless one day it so happened that one of my close friends from my village who was earlier quite brilliant but had now been relegated to the third or fourth position with my sudden elevation to the top in ranks in the class, felt disenchanted with the classes, to some extent, due to *Bhaagadbhoot*'s strictness. There was no such problem with me although. My friend suggested that we go to the market instead of attending the classes. I suspected his intentions first, but when he said that we would come back soon, I thought it as part of cordiality and good behaviour to accompany him, although I was fearing that our teacher would notice it and would beat us or punish us. What phantom had taken my friend that he persisted in his indulgence and I followed in his shoes foolishly!

After having sauntered around for a while in the market, we reached a lathe machine whose owner or artisan or mechanic, whatever you call him, was possibly known to my friend and his father by some distant relationship. After discussing some nonsensical topics, the wily adult proposed that we help him in revolving the lathe wheel, to which my friend agreed very enthusiastically; I however did not. I was more concerned about my classes that we had bunked, and my teacher; I was a star of my class, how could I bunk my classes! But my friend had no such qualms: he had nothing to lose; he was not the star of the class. It was my foolishness to follow him – a non-star -- in his errands, in his loafing. He did not agree to go back to school and we bunked the further sessions. The lathe owner agreed to pay us 25 *paise* for our labours. Per day! We thus became labourers at the lathe machine. Child labourers! When his job was done, the lathe man did not give us the promised money – the *chavannee* -- on the promise that he would pay when large amount was accumulated. And my friend became happier that he would get a huge sum one day if he continued to do this menial job, forgetting the studies, the education, for which he did come from the village to the town daily. And out of my foolishness I, too, had been caught in the trap without any earnestness on my part.

Nevertheless, I felt a strong sense of guilt and horror that my education was being bartered for an errand of a cunning mechanic of lathe machine. We left our bags in the school only and collected at the time of closing of the school. First day, nobody took notice of our absence, possibly thinking that we might have got to do some shopping, essential shopping in the nearby *baazaar.*

But like a bad habit, my friend again repeated the same thing the next day, and then the next day, and in the process, for about four days, and was very happy that he had started earning money, which was the prime aim of all the education and of the life *per se.* Why I got indulged, I don't know; I might be lacking my own decision-making powers, I think. But I was constantly gnawed by my guilt conscience. Fourth day, when my friend insisted for payment of our dues, the cunning mechanic refused to pay saying that he would pay at week-end. We smelled something fishy in his intentions and got disillusioned and decided to give up the debut earning venture. Dejected, we returned to our school: my friend morose, yet I was happy that this way I was out of the trap of the lathe man, and of my foolish and money-blinded friend, too.

As soon as we reached the school gate, the students shouted, "*Maassaab*, they are there!"

In fact, they were on the lookout for both of us for all those four days when we were bunking the classes. The teacher ordered us to be captured. Frightened, we were presented before the scary personality of *Bhaagadbhoot.* He sternly asked us where we had been for all those four days. We were liars and had no qualms about lying, and therefore told in meek voices that we had some important jobs in some relative's house in the town. The seasoned teacher despite being fully conscious that we were lying did not punish us and instructed sternly that from next day we should be present in the school lest we should be beaten badly. I was happy internally and was cursing my friend for making me party to his misdeeds, yet I was amazed at the magnanimity of the reputably strict teacher. He was in fact a soft-hearted person, however, deigning to be tough outwardly so as to discipline the kids. I realised this fact that day. I took a vow never to follow any such friend in his misdeeds and misadventures in future.

Even today, this seemingly insignificant incident haunts me at night, and in my dreams I face nightmares and shudder at the thought that I am bunking the class and would fail. I get out of this terror only when I wake up and realise that I am no more a student now. That I have crossed all those boundaries and am presently reaping the fruits of my deeds – *karmas* -- both good and bad.

XXX

Table of Contents

9. Literacy And Breach Of Decency

Enter Mother

The other day, my son posed a question to me, "Why are our elder grandfather – *Chhote Daadaa* – and our elder aunt – *Taaee* – not on talking terms, not even our elder uncle – *Taaujee* – is on talking terms with him and his entire family? We share the *Khedaa* with them, with half of the area occupied by them and the other half by us?"

"Well, that's true: they are not on talking terms! There is an ugly tale behind this fact. The outcomes of life and social set-up are the results of a long chain of incidents taking place unintentionally, however, seemingly being done deliberately as well as on purpose by our adversaries.

"A couple of years back, at our households, there was some repair work going on; those were the days of monsoon and the habitats, constructed of *kutcha* clay and soil and having reed-thatches as terraces, were susceptible to damage during torrents of the monsoon rains."

"Why were there no pucca constructions, despite our being rich and influential people?", my smart son interjected.

"I don't know exactly why. Why; however, that may be owing to the practice of those days, nobody was having faith in having pucca habitats, or in having permanent dwellings. Those were the days of strife and struggles and bloody fights; when people had to flee from one place to another along with their entire household and establishment sometimes. May be that was the motivating factor behind not having pucca or permanent structures, that is houses. Nothing was sure and certain in those days; everything was transient! Ever in a flux!", I laughed concluding my remark.

"But ephemeral and impermanent it still is.." interposed my son again, albeit in a philosophical manner and with metaphysical undertones.

"Quite unlike the uncertainty of those medieval days, when even life's continuance was not certain, even for the next day!", I clarified. My son, living in the times of peace in modern days, had no idea about the medieval times of war, tumult and strife. Only recently, the country had had a tryst with bloodbath wherein tens of millions of countrymen had been displaced, butchered, raped and mutilated like those by daemons and monsters, in the name of getting 'Freedom' which in fact was another misnomer for the transfer of power from the Britishers to their stooges –

the dynasty in the making, the would-be fiefdom, courtesy of the sham sage who got the title of the 'Father of the Nation' in return for this favour to the aspiring or, if one likes to call it, the greedy would-be dynasty.

"Nonetheless, somehow, a sense of *déjà vu* had set in amongst the citizenry with the exodus of Britishers, and they had started thinking that thenceforth everything would be hunky dory for them, and that nobody would force them to leave their habitats any more like during medieval days."

"But, still people have been forced to leave their habitats where they had been living for millennia: *Kashmeer* is the glaring example! It makes little difference whether it was Britisher or an Indian a ruler.", my son remarked with a tinge of irritability and pique.

"Agreed! As regards the state of citizenry, nothing much has changed!", I pacified my son by concurring with his views. However, I continued my narrative of the causative factor of enmity between our two blood-related families.

"The artisan who was working at ours needed a better spade; of course, he had one already, but that was not working, even as, it had got blunted by constant use. He demanded another spade – a sharpened one.

"It was not a big issue; in a village spade should not be such a big issue; every peasant possesses spades and shovels; and has in multiple numbers; it's such an important implement of agricultural pursuits. Your elder aunt finding you loitering thereabout – you were fascinated by the repair work going on and were watching how it was being done – caught hold of you – for the ladies were not supposed to venture out of the households or do any manual job as the picking of a spade or any small implement from outside the precincts of their house – and she instructed you to go to our *Khedaa* and bring the other spade which was kept there in the hall on our side of the *Khedaa*. However, you departed with some hesitation and with a quizzical look on your countenance muttering that you did not know what '*Faavda*' (Spade) meant, to which, the aunt showed the blunt spade lying there, and you were obliged to do the errand come what may. And come it did eventually, as the episode that unfolded in its wake would disclose.

"Within no time you were back! Your aunt saw the spade and remarked that the same was not our spade, yet was content that the job was small and the spade would be returned soon, and that someone might have given you that spade. She gave the spade to the construction artisan.

"In fact, you had picked up

the spade being used nearby at the repair site of *Chhote Daadaa*'s household. Unbeknown to them and to their labourers, you picked up the implement, put it on your small shoulders and came back jolly happily having accomplished the tough task so smoothly.

"There ensued a search in the wake of this unintentional theft for the implement at the site of the theft. Someone had made away with the spade! At the crucial time when it was required so badly! As the fate would have it, in the meantime the job at our site had been finished and the spade was to be replenished at its proper place. And by now the elder son of your aunt – your elder cousin -- had come back from where he had been sent, and was asked to return the spade to *Daadaa*'s site. This time not you but your cousin was assigned the task, for he was bigger and capable of handling the heavy implement easily; therefore, he gladly agreed to do the errand. You were small and were facing difficulty in lifting the heavy implement, you were of such a young age!

"No sooner had your cousin reached the site of *Chhote Daadaa* with the spade on his shoulders gleefully, not suspecting the incidents to come immediately thereafter, than the *Daadaa* shouted, '*Eh*, so it's you, rascal, the thief! Here we are searching for the spade and you have made away with the essential implement, even without asking us for?' And an intemperate adult as he ever was he slapped the adolescent boy in the face. Your cousin was also not sort of a boy who could take such affronts lying down, nor was his mother, your elder aunt. He shouted back, too, and tried to clarify that he had not taken away the spade, also that rather he had come to return the same instead; but *Daadaa* was *daadaa*, a beast incarnate, he added some more slaps to the earlier stock on the chubby and cherub cheeks of the lad.

"Your cousin rushed towards the home in extreme rage and poured his fury against his mother, your aunt. Your aunt is a literate and educated lady and of open mind. She was adapting to the feudal set-up but was never comfortable with the suffocating atmosphere prevalent therein. Nonetheless, she was considered to be a bold lady, therefore a 'bad lady' by implication; they liked submissive, uneducated, illiterate and slavish type of ladies in those feudal set ups. Your aunt shouted a war cry and rushed towards the scene of offence – it was hardly ten feet away. She uncovered her face, removed her veil – an unprecedented happening in the annals of feudal family, and used the foulest language against the *Daadaa,* who was thus far an invincible warlord, a furious icon of the family. Your aunt had in this fashion sort of challenged *Daadaa*'s insuperable authority. She used all sorts of invectives and humiliating phrases denting the image and goodwill of *Daadaa* for good. Your cousin was alongside her in the obscene and foul-mouthed quarrel and did contribute fuel to the fire of ire and angst of the lady.

"The culprit were you! You were terrified at this turn of events at such a trifling incident – of using the implement of same family by same family only. What sort of relationship was this? Moreover, you were at fault, but the punishment was meted out to your cousin without giving any thought to find out the real culprit. You were scared to think that if it were found out later on that it was you who had taken away the spade, you would be the centre of wrath of both the parties. In fact, your aunt was also not aware that the spade was picked from the site of *Daadaa*, otherwise she would not have used it; she knew the nature and temperament of *Daadaa.* However, the fate would have it otherwise!

"For high decibels were being used on both the sides, and other family members of *Daadaa* had also joined in the ugly imbroglio, very foul scene unbecoming of the respectable family had been created there, and the entire village gathered around there, and came to know of the declining fortunes and fate of the one-time high as well decent family. This was yet another ominous event!

"Not only this, when your elder uncle – the husband of your aunt came at the week-end, he also fought an obscene battle of words with the entire family of *Daadaa.* The bizarre thing was that the entire group was living inside the same compound of habitat, the same *Baakhar*; and with such enmity how long could they live and co-exist!

"*Badee Ammaa* – the eldest grandmother - was still there alive; the wife of *Daadaa* was there too, alive at that time. All were stunned! The limit of decorum and decency had been breached! And in its worst possible manner! How to set right an unbridled lady? The blame was put squarely on the part of education, the lettering, the literacy: of ladies. The illiterate and uneducated ladies of the household behaved meekly and submissively and could never have breached the line of demarcation between the brute authority or chivalry of male fiefdom. The elder aunt – *taaee* -- became stained for ever thereafter. Nor did she care for anybody thereafter, too. Her feminine masculinity was not liked by anybody including myself."

"What was the reaction of our suave and seasoned grandfather;

he was so close to *Daadaa* and they sat together in the evening at the winter bonfire? And what was the stand of our father? Did he take sides with his sister-in-law, the wife of his elder brother, or with *Daadaa* with whom he had an affectionate bond?", my son queried.

"Your *Baabaa* was pained to learn of this ugly episode. He could not say anything to his daughter-in-law for he was dependent on her household for two morsels of food. In fact your grandfather had very erroneous attitude towards life. He never considered it necessary that for living a respectable life it is essential for the living being – most of all the human beings – to arrange for food, clothing and shelter personally first of all, and also, one should develop some social clout and should endeavour to grow it gradually to keep up with the fast changing times, lest one should be left behind and ultimately discarded, even humiliated helplessly, as your grandfather was finding himself in that situation, of late, at his advanced age. He was caught in a time-warp: he started with a feudal upbringing and a life of riches, and he fixed this frame in his mind for good. He could not take cognizance of the exodus of Britishers on whom the entire feudal well-being of his and his wealthy and renowned relatives was pivoted. Besides, he did not take stock of this factor of

paramount importance, the money; he neglected money totally and, in the process, lost esteem in society; for society was evolving entirely along the lines of accumulation of money, to the neglect of all other factors, like prestige or education or social standing. All those old criteria had been hinged on only one factor thenceforth – the money! Post *British Raj*!"

"Our *Baabaajee* is not our grandfather in the same sense as the other grandfathers are to their grandchildren!" My son averred, to which, when I quizzically looked towards him, he added, "He in fact cannot help us in any respect, least of all, monetarily, as an ideal relationship, particularly, that of a grandparent and grandchildren should be: one's grandparent ought to be capable of supporting one's grandchildren in every respect, to stake claim to that lofty relationship!"

I agreed yet could not add a word to this bold thinking.

"It was learnt later on that on the day of the despicable episode, *Baabaa* had sat at the bonfire as usual along with his elder cousin – *Daadaa* – and is said to have made the remark, "That is why the wise of the old have suggested that a wise man should never argue with a lady! *(Bade boodhon kaa kahnaa hai ki baiyarbaaniyon ke munh nahin lagnaa chaahiye!)*" Only that much! *Daadaa* held him in very high regard ever since his days in *B R College, Aagaraa,* when he was there along with the latter's own younger brother, since deceased.

"As regards your father, he was never a votary of his sister-in-law; he openly criticized her *Bhaabhee* for her brazenness and supported *Daadaa* without any qualms. After this incident, nonetheless, the two broader families were sequestered and did never patch up. Despite living in the same compound! How suffocating it would have been, you can just imagine!", I concluded.

XXX

Table of Contents

10. Nayaa Daur *And My Adventurism*

Enter Protagonist

Life is not all chastity! Life is not all agriculture, or business, or service, or play, or festivities, or schooling! On the upper surface of society these aspects of life are perceptible, visible and most of the ignoramuses take it for the be all and end all of life on this planet; our Earth. Apart from financial and existential aspects of life, there is a constant current of sex and sensuality which runs underneath all these facets of social life and becomes the base of all other aspects, even as, it affects them all.

At that tender age, too, all sorts of obscene activities were indulged in by the kids; and stories concerning this topic did circulate among little kids, true or false, unbeknown to all. One such gossip was that a particular boy of higher age as compared to ours was indulged in such profane activity along with a boy of younger age who was given over by the mother of the younger boy to the elder boy for accompanying the former to the school in the genuine hope that the elder one would behave morally and ethically. However, the creation does not run on the lines of peoples' assumptions, that is, ethics; Nature has its own formulae and chemistry and biology that work insuperably and preponderantly. Given the opportunity, only that tendency prevails overpowering all other considerations and man-made strictures, relationships or trusts that the Nature has dispensed. Deluge of lust and libido when aroused dismantles all sorts of ethical boundaries, smashes all sorts of considerations, and inundates every possible semblance of morality so assiduously tried to be set in the society.

Breach of trust it might be dubbed, yet unbeknown to the elders and particularly to the mother of the innocent little child! I learnt a lesson in this episode in that elders must never trust to the children of elder ages the custody or the care-taking of those of younger ages: the animal instinct of sensuality would overpower them and defile the character of both.

In those days, schools were not aided by Govt and they were sort of private institutions, sort of *zameendaaree,* allegorically. With the *zameendaaree* having been abolished, the astute well off and rich people devised this novel tool of perpetuating *zameendaaree* in *neo* format, that of opening schools and earning money just like they did in *zameendaaree* system. Here, the owners or founders of schools earned money regularly in the shape of fees and in the shape of 'cut' from the already meagre salary of the teachers who were normally *ad hoc* teachers, always hand to mouth. At the town, the school where my father used to teach as an *ad hoc* teacher of English was also owned by one erstwhile *zameendaar;* claiming himself to be a *Braahman,* but indulged in all such sins and improprieties.

Nevertheless, to augment and strengthen the financial spine of the school, or it may also be said, to support the school monetarily, the schools everywhere used to organise at frequent intervals some cultural functions, like *Nautankee,* Theatre, Cinema, Concerts of regional singers etc. These were not in tandem with their ethical conceptions and they felt qualms of conscience in organising such events, too, yet the need for money predominated the ethics and morals. One such event was organised by the town school that year and the stuff to offer the audience was the cinema: shows of films – old films. A makeshift cinema hall made of curtains was created in the bivouacs and the audience were permitted to watch it for ticket. Cinema was a great attraction and a novelty for the rural folk, that too, in the town, even as, the same was to be projected without a cinema hall or screen! It was to be projected merely onto a cloth curtain. There was great buzz all around about this cinema event brought home; something extraordinary was happening in the town! The school was earning fairly sumptuously by this event.

We kids also came to learn about it; we belonged to the town too, though to the primary school only! My father was a teacher in the bigger school; I should be privileged to watch cinema free of cost on this score, otherwise what was the use of my being the son of a teacher! We, almost half a dozen children, made a plan: to watch the cinema. The cinema on the day to be shown was *'Nayaa Daur'* as we were told. We kids did not know even what the term *Nayaa* signified, nor what the term *Daur* meant; still we decided firmly to watch the cinema. The same lad of advanced age was our leader who was doing fouls with the another young innocent yet wealthy lad without the knowledge of his parents, especially, mother. For a while I felt hesitant to accompany this group of lads fearing that he might do the same harm to us all too on the way; after all, the town was two and half kilometres away, and it was all wilderness in between, rendering the distance seemingly equivalent to thousand kilometres in the night as well as dusk. The wilderness could not be measured in normal kilometres, its every inch equalled a kilometre, especially, when it came to such depraved activities, or plunder or murders on the way. And our area was not an exception to all that like all the rest countryside!

Still, we ventured out and almost half a dozen lads proceeded towards the town in the darkness or dusk or just thereafter. We were moving merrily chatting all sorts of nonsense and cherishing the prospect of watching cinema for the first time in our lifetimes: at such a tender age! We were given the feedback that '*Nayaa Daur*' was the 'best' movie of the time. And of the world!

Anyway, we reached the town, passed by our *Aadarsh Paathshaalaa* and reached the school of our father. My elder cousin was also with me, that is why I was confident that no harm would be done to me since in the past also he had rescued us kids from the profanities of a rascal in the sugarcane field. No such thing, however, happened fortunately this time. Nevertheless, I was constantly gnawed by the fear that if my father came to know of my sojourn to the town in the night, he would not only reprimand me, but also, flog my innocent mother, who had all along been forbidding me from going to town with the naughty and depraved boys. However, I drew solace in the idea that my father would be in the school and would not come back home that night, and also, that we should not be sighted by him in the crowd. Thus there would be no question of his coming to know of all this – our first time adventurism.

Throughout the way to the town I was suggesting to the leading lad that we should not meet our father there, but he thought entirely differently in that it depended on our father's clout only that they could get the free entry to the show. They were in fact banking upon my resources, that is, my father's clout in the school. Thus, in their perspective, there was no question of our not meeting our father.

They went straight to the teachers' room at the school. My father was present there; we wished him somewhat hesitantly. He also got surprised at our adventurism, but did not get angry or upset, amazingly for me. He rather welcomed us – me and my cousin – thinking that we had come without knowledge of our mothers, having been instigated by the urchins of the village. He introduced us to his fellow teachers and made us pay regards to them, too. We were now in safe hands, in which we were not thus far.

As we, along with teachers and fellow students from our village, were merry-making in the teachers' room, an idea struck one of our group members, a somewhat elder student; he suggested, "*Maassaab*, if we brought sugarcanes from the nearby fields, what a relishing feast it would be?"

The teachers were but rustic villagers, they permitted the lads but sounded that their theft should not be disclosed to the owner of the field; the owner was from a martial race. The lads assured the teachers and left for the dignified and adventurous feat, that is, theft. After sometime they came with loads of sugarcanes carried on an upturned cot, a heavy assortment of sugarcanes. To the bewilderment of consenting teachers!

"Why have you brought so much load? You were asked to bring only a few sugarcanes – half a dozen at the most?"

"But *Maassaab*, there are so many people! Moreover, the owner of the field is a very rich farmer, he is not going to be a pauper with this much theft!"

All of them relished the sugarcanes. However, when they had almost finished, the owner of the sugarcane field arrived at the scene and complained to the teachers that their students had damaged his sugarcane crop badly; they had not only taken the canes, but also, felled smashed a large number of canes in the process.

However, the teachers denied the episode outright; they said, "It's not possible. These lads are students of our school, very gentle and disciplined; they cannot indulge in such bad activities, we are sure!" My father too shielded the lads. What could the poor hapless farmer do when the teachers themselves were vouchsafing a falsehood as truth!

Thereafter, when the dust had settled on the episode of sugarcane theft and the victim had departed grumbling, and the thieves set free, we thought that the cinema would eventually start and we would watch the same in company with our father and other teachers. However, that was not to be. Our father and one other teacher – our father's colleague and friend -- proposed that we and those two teachers would go to the residence of yet another colleague teacher of the town itself and stay overnight there only. We went there; the stay was cozy, beyond our expectations and eligibility, for our legs, hands and clothes were all dirt-ridden and all smeared. And the coverlets and floors of the house were very clean and tidy befitting gentlemen guests. However, the hosts were kind to us and not fastidious. We were grumbling that we did not get to watch the cinema for which we had taken so much trouble and risk!

In the morning, we got up early and accompanied our father towards our village silently. Our father also made no fuss about our adventurism and the negligence of our mothers in having allowed us to go to the town in the night exposing ourselves to so much risk. It was another miracle and puzzle for us! Unprecedented in the annals of my father's life!

XXX

Table of Contents

11. Amongst The Elders: First Photograph

Enter Father

While studying at *Aadarsh Paathshaalaa*, my son – by that time he was the only son of mine, albeit later in life I got two more – one day happened to visit my school accompanying some children of somewhat higher age hailing from our village only. The lads were under the impression that my son being my son would be welcomed at my school warmly by the fellow teachers and the students, I being an influential person in the school. He was quite a little kid at that time.

They found me out, and my son became glad to see me at school. Being a small child and totally innocent, my son was glad to have achieved this mile stone: of visiting his father's school. I felt pleased and happy, too, to see my little son in my school. My love towards my little kid oozed out and I introduced him to my fellow teachers and made him to bow down in obeisance to the venerable *gurus*, my co-teachers in fact.

The time was evening time and the occasion incidentally that day was that of farewell party being organised for the Matriculation students who were soon to take their exams and leave the school for higher colleges and other places, or even simply to drop out . There was lot of activity going on all around there in the school at the moment. The students were busy making preparations: laying chairs and tables in cascading arrangement for students to stand on and chairs in front row for teachers to sit in.

Some students from our village caught sight of my son and they became glad to see a little kid in their midst. They took charge of my son and started playing with him and entertaining him.

The town's photographer who had come from another small city was busy setting up his huge sized rudimentary camera in the compound at a proper distance. The camera was to be mounted on a tripod of height about six or seven feet and was to be covered with a black cloth so as not to expose it to extraneous light while taking photographs. Its grating was opened for certain number of seconds only, and only a dexterous cameraman could do the job perfectly. Those were not the days of modern day automatic and coloured cameras. They used to be merely black and white impressions, that too, after having been properly developed inside some dark-room of the cameraman's studio, or in some other professional's studio, far away in the town or the small city.

My son was agape gazing at the magic box, that was camera hidden under a black cloak like a *Muslim* lady wearing *burqaa*. His caretakers or entertainers told my son that they were preparing to take photograph of the group. When everything got ready, I removed the son to one side; he was not a high school student. Nonetheless, the fellow teachers and students suggested to take my son also amidst the group of students for taking photograph. Thus was my small son taken into the group of passing out students of High School. And he was stupefied and mesmerized to see all this wizardry being done when the students told

him that his image would be taken on the distant camera. He marvelled at the magic how his replica of the countenance could be taken at such a distance without using pen or pencil or crayon. However, that is what science is all about and which the ignoramuses dub as miracle or magic! In this bizarre Creation in fact there in no miracle, no magic at all; all is based on cause and effect, we may or may not fathom the same, notwithstanding. The photograph was taken. And we reached home. My son was fearing that I would be displeased that he had been to school to my embarrassment before the entire school faculty, but it was not so.

On reaching home, my son conveyed this seventh wonder to his mother very enthusiastically, "*Beebee*! My *photoo* has been taken! Along with tenth class students! *Photoo*!"

"*Pitaajee*, shall I get to see my *photoo*?", he enquired of me.

"Yes!"

In due course, of course, I procured one copy of the group photograph for the sake of my son, for that was his first ever photograph. On the plate of photo amidst the students, there was a little kid sitting cross-legged, however, with two front teeth exposed as if wondering on this new found glory for himself! I handed the photograph to him and his mother and remarked mockingly, "He has been photographed with his mouth agape and teeth exposed!"

"Just like small children! In awe!", his mother counterbalanced my insensitive utterance.

My son was taking my remark as a derision, a criticism of his failure in giving a proper pose, but the fact was that the childish pose was all the more attractive. However, with this photograph of my son with tenth grade students, my son got under the inexorable impression that he was now a tenth class student himself, as a proof of which, he now had at hand a group photograph. That's how child psychology works!

Nevertheless, for qualifying the fearsome Matriculation exam and for becoming a Matriculate, one has to burn plentiful of midnight oil; only then can one become eligible for that prestige. My son took time to grasp this nuanced knowledge. Even my father and his cousin had not been able to qualify the Matriculation exam and lived a *lack-a-daisical* life unbecoming of his stature of a scion of an illustrious family. And I? I did graduation, yet to what avail! My son kept on putting up this poser to me throughout remainder of my life when the train of time had bypassed me with my cumbersome baggage of failures, specifically, in picking up the qualification of B.Ed. for securing a teaching, the basic knowledge of arithmetic and mathematics for living *per se*, and the knowledge of Geography a prerequisite for securing a Govt job at that time; as was also pointed out to me by many worthies in later life on analysis of my career graph by them.

XXX

Table of Contents

12. Childish Theft And Paradise Lost

Enter Protagonist

One can never recover from one's *karmas*! The fact that I am still today recollecting this seemingly innocuous incident with a sense of guilt as well as sigh of regret and compunction is proof enough of my conviction. I was in class three, the repeat year of class three, even as, I had been retained in class three for one extra year by my father on purpose. My goodwill was very high although. I was a brilliant lad of the school. Teachers praised me and the fellow mates were under awe of mine. *Chiranjee* had reconciled to the reality, too, given my unassuming countenance whereby I betrayed no ill-will towards him, rather, I always greeted him affectionately and in a child-like manner. I was wallowing in the glow of my glory, found providentially, rather, accidentally. I was myself amazed at this bounty of Creator, the Almighty, however, showered on me undeservingly, as I perceived it!

One day, all at once, in the afternoon, we kids were sitting in our class, in the veranda of the school, without any task at hand or without any lessons being taught by our teachers. Even the teachers were not free to teach us; they were engaged with senior students. We kids were therefore getting bored due to the lack of activity. It's only the activity that keeps living beings happy and at ease, lest one should become restive and ill at ease. Even the sages of *Upanishad* era have pronounced this fact: *'Kurvanneveh karmaani jijeevishech-chhatam samah!'* (Meaning thereby, with a view to being able to sustain one's life, one must needs to get oneself constantly busy in some task or the other.)

It was the period of late afternoon. Life do itself is so weary; on top of that, the sitting idle in the school is as though the climax of that ennui. The teachers, or masters as they dub them, in such schools are seen more interested in keeping the kids under tab and discipline than to teach or instruct them something worthwhile or creative; unmindful of whether their own callousness results in breaking the morale and psychic sanity of the impressionable kids. This reflects in every action of theirs, for instance, even if they take the children for outing – on picnic – the kids are commanded ludicrously to hold the hands of one another and then to move ahead. Now, in this tortuous situation, wherein one of the hands is being pulled by the schoolmate from behind and the other one by the playmate from the front, what the hell of a picnicking would one be enjoying! Nevertheless, only this is the invariable scenario being played and imposed on the pitiable toddlers in schools, with the result that when there must be an energised and effusive countenance of children at the end of the trip, every child at the end of the picnic is seen in a state of utter weariness and state of lowest stamina, what to speak of morose countenance. At times, in such a scenario, some students fall sick, too.

Almost alike was the day for us wretched kids, the students; it wasn't a picnic exactly yet the teachers were engrossed in chit-chatting and gossiping with their colleagues, after having commanded the class that every soul must sit silently lest their legs would be snapped by beating if they ventured or dared to move them even an inch from their original position. Also, that they would be transfixed in the pose of a cock. Silence, everybody! No noise, no mischief, no nuisance! For the teachers were gossiping beside!

Queer and weird command without any doubt! In fact here onward only this teacher was vested with the duty to teach the class; therefore the fate of the class was decided: to sit alike a boulder or lump of stone, without moving the limbs till it was time to call it quits. Leave apart the innocent kids, even if a *Yogee* were commanded alike to sit in this posture for so long, one would cringe and might even cry! The Creation – the Nature – has created every iota of the living organs conscious, moveable, intended to be in a perennial state of movement, without stopping for a moment even. Lack of motion even for a moment may result in the organ turning defunct or dead. Not only this, even a seemingly inert and immobile mountain likes to move, the mother earth too likes to move – and does move, not only stir, it does sprint in the limitless sky at a dazzling as well as unimaginable speed of nearly 30 kms per second, and that too perennially; this is the reality of all-pervading phenomena of 'motions', not to talk of unmentionably trifling and insignificant desire to move on the part of living beings! Moreover, when it's an earthquake or tornado, the entire cosmos seems to be shuddering and moving!

However, it seems, the teachers get their wages merely for keeping the kids – the prospective assets of the nation -- under tabs and strict discipline – brooking no distraction or diversion, in a static discipline.

How many teachers are there who can fathom the complex mysteries of the evolution or development of the minds of *homo sapiens*? On top of that, the vocation of teaching is picked by only those souls who would otherwise have been rejected by the society or the system for any better vocation or better job. It can also be said in other words that the teacher is a residuum, a leftover, of all the resources of humanity. Nevertheless, the irony is that in the composition of creation or the society the most crucial duty – the duty of formation and evolution of humankinds, the responsibility of evolution of appropriate human beings for the future – is assigned to these dregs of society only.

For the most crucial job concerning society, the least worthy resources are deployed! The residuum of the stock of intellect! The dregs of IQ! The leftover of virtues! Meaning thereby, a human being possesses the virtues like dynamism, intellect, reliability *et al;* however, a teacher's job only the one is destined to get who lacks all these virtues. For, if one would be endowed with all these virtues worthy of humanity, one would get a better job somewhere else, at a better option. He would become an IAS, first of all; or he would become an Engineer somewhere; or a financial manager in some good firm, and the like. The long and short of it is that the vocation of teaching is taken up only by one who is not a human species of best or better quality. This is the reality of teaching job, the hypocrisy of regarding the *Gurus* as gods, notwithstanding! They are not real *Gurus!*

If there is no worthwhile task at hand to do, one tempts to make mischief to kill the time. I never indulged in mischief making and was considered to be a gentle guy without an iota of doubt whatsoever. Nevertheless, a child is a child! If one does not make noise or does not make mischief, it does not necessarily mean that one can't! Or one doesn't have the potential for!

I too alike the cog in a defunct machine – whose operator as though had deserted it and gone to chat with his freak accomplices after switching the machine off -- was squatted at the floor as did all other classmates. Otherwise too, a teacher is a very cruel creature; the students, therefore, have no other option but to blindly obey his commands, both sensible and insensible.

All the children were getting wearied by squatting without any activity at hand. Some of them were sleeping and some others dozing off. Some were peering hither whilst others were gazing thither. Extreme ennui! At that age we kids were yet not conversant with the nomenclature of such sort of a feeling. It was only quite late in life that we came to understand that every feeling of the mind and heart of a human being has been assigned a very attractive as well as meaningful appellation. 'Weariness' or 'boredom' is one such enchanting word which has the traits such as it can be used anywhere, under any sort of circumstances; for instance, if someone is not to one's liking, 'the person is bore', if the lecture is not to one's liking, 'the speaker or lecturer is bore', if one does not have anything worthwhile to dispense, 'oneself is getting bored'. Likewise, we kids were getting extremely bored.

Boredom is utterly unbearable a state by nature. Nonetheless, it can be undone quite easily too, for which, however, an ample amount of common sense is warranted on the part of the sufferer. I for one set off on a thought process that something interesting be done to break the monotony of sitting listlessly along with the static class so that the students might feel like moving their organs and activating their brains, in the process generating fun, which in all probability would be a better proposition than the dreariness of the period.

As already mentioned, majority of the children were dozing, or were unalert. They were innocent kids, unaware of the vices of the world of living beings on the planet yet. I peeked around and found that none was looking towards me.

I did squat cross-legged beside a gentle lad from my own village, and he was quite a favourite of mine. To ward off the weariness and the drudgery of the day, I don't know why, I stumbled upon a wily plan: I stealthily picked the inkpot of my neighbour and hid it under my leg. Simply as a prank! My idea was to enjoy the prank and laugh it off in the process and eventually to return the inkpot; sort of sense of humour.

Well, stealthily I picked the inkpot of the student sitting beside me and hid it below my thigh. It is for sure that I had no absolute intention of indulging in the nefarious pursuit of theft; I merely intended to implement my fancy for generating sense of humour by enacting a scene of weirdness. I had initially intended to replace the inkpot to the neighbour after putting him to some botheration about his petty loss.

Ved Prakaash, this was the name of the boy, my neighbour; simpleton only, alike myself; the fact is that all the children and toddlers are gentle and innocent only! After accomplishing this task verging on theft, a chuckle did appear on my countenance; more so thinking that because *Ved Prakaash* was dozing at that moment, he would not come to know of the fact of my having stolen his inkpot. 'Now the ignorant one would understand what it costs to doze in the class', I thought.

But it was not to be! However, the things did not pan out as per my supposition. Entire of my plan went astray.

I kept sitting like a fool. For some time, my friend did not take cognizance of my mischief as well as the disappearance of his inkpot mysteriously and all at once. After sometime, almost at the nick of the hour when we were about to leave the school, he realised that his inkpot was not there.

The final bell proclaiming end of the day had been rung and I got perplexed. *Ved Prakaash* too woke up and not finding his inkpot in place got anxious shouting, "Oh! My inkpot?"

He exclaimed, "What about my inkpot? It was here! *Oooo!*"

I had entered the *Chakravyooh* somehow but now I found myself entrapped within it, figuratively alike *Abhimanyu* of *Mahaabhaarat* renown, finding no way out of it; I didn't have that acumen alike *Abhimanyu* only who had no acumen to come out of the *Chakravyooh* of seven warriors. I thus had failed in successfully executing my project of merry-making.

For a moment, he threw a penetrating gaze at me, but immediately took it aside declaring that it couldn't be me for sure; he was so confident of my honesty and integrity. I felt abashed. But how off the mark he was! He declared explicitly before the class that I could never indulge in such mean action as stealing an inkpot, "It can't be you! For sure!"

I still offered, "Do search, maybe!" in the hope and with the intention that if he would conduct a search rummaging through my bag he would find the inkpot and I would divulge the entire gameplan of having fun with him.

But he deserted me after reposing misplaced trust in me – a thief – saying, "Leave it, it can't be with you. I know who might be having stolen the same!"

He could not imagine in his wildest dreams that I – such a gem of a child -- could steal his inkpot. When he came to me, I kept sitting like a duffer would, bearing a foolish countenance as if I did know nothing. The credulous guy came to me and I felt as if that was my last bastion of prestige that was going to be dismantled. Luckily, my goodwill came to my rescue, even as, my volition would have worked, for I did not intend in my heart to steal

the inkpot, and intended to ultimately replace it, so the boy did not search my bag and merely cursorily checked my satchel and moved on commenting 'You can't do that!'. I was relieved: of a grave mishap. Had I been caught, I would have been branded as a thief for all the future incidents of theft in the class, whether I committed those or not. A bad name is worse than a bad man *(Bad achchhaa badnaam buraa!)*

It was decided after some discourse and discussion, as was the convention prevalent, to search the bags of the kids, for kids kept their stolen exploits in the bags unmindful of the fact that the first thing if the search was undertaken would be the bags only. I had hidden the same not in the bag but under the leg, for my intention was not to steal but to have fun and play prank on my friend. I got scared having been caught in my own trap, even as, the ingenuous child started rummaging through the bags of children from the far end of the row of students.

And then ensued the rummaging through the bags of the kids. The boy searched the bags of those boys with particular intensity on whom he had suspicion. But inkpot was not to be found; how could it? For he had already absolved the real thief of the crime and whom he was considering as a saint.

I got immersed in the deep

sense of guilt: extreme guilt conscience! I had failed miserably in my debut fun project. Now, in the changed circumstances, I could not gather courage even to declare that I had stolen the pot merely for fun's sake; now when the hilarious mishap of theft had been broadcasted amongst the entire class, it would have been permanently detrimental to my goodwill, had I divulged the truth at that juncture: the classmates would have lost faith in my righteousness for good. I therefore considered it expedient to keep mum as regards the mystery of the incident. I realised, too, in this process that a person having turned a thief or scoundrel does start gaining expertise in the art of cunning and falsehood, the lies. In other words, the 'intelligence' is but the euphemism for cunning, falsehood, theft and stealth!

Meanwhile, the school bell had been rung and in the melee, the students rushed out, picking up their bags disregarding the ongoing project of search. The school time was up and the students were in the mood to flee impatiently. *Ved* did forsake the episode, too, including the concern for inkpot, exclaiming, "Oh, damnit, I'll buy another one!" and slinging the satchel on his little shoulders he ran away, too. It was me who got up in the end, with a guilty conscience, for I had to take

care so as to put the stolen ware from beneath my thighs into the satchel avoiding it being noticed by anybody. However, the chances of being watched were remote, for everybody was desperate to run away alike the calves kept aloof from their cow mothers for the day!

I, too, deftly as well as clandestinely pushed the inkpot into my bag and rushed towards my home, however, repenting the ill-episode and misadventure I had embarked upon. Thereafter, I decided never to ever play pranks on my fellow friends either in class or in office, for this was the first and the last time that I had been forgiven by Providence, and my prestige and goodwill had been salvaged by my *karmas*. For future, however, there was no guarantee that I would be spared if I repeated the misdeed.

Nevertheless, this seemingly trifling episode, on the happening and conclusion of which I didn't have my own control, left an indelible imprint or stain on my conscience for ever, and very deep one. That regret I still feel! Even after lapse of several decades, or more than half a century!

Throughout the way to my village, I kept on regretting my unintentional action that turned out to be a foolish *faux pas* in the end, and might turn out to be a permanent undoing of my entire illustrious performance; I was after all a proclaimed saint, a certified gifted scholar of the school, and on top of that, the son of an influential teacher of another school, a higher school. Alas, I could rewind the incident as well as the time! But time is inelastic; it can't be replayed, there is no U-turn in time's journey or velocity, except in the machine of memory. In memory, nonetheless, it persists for ever!

However, unhurt I had come out of this seemingly innocuous incident of sin and unethical act, I could never get rid of my guilt conscience ever since. Even if one's intentions are mirthful, the actions may turn out to be quite hazardous for life's trajectory in society! How many plain-hearted and innocent as well as ignorant children get punished and branded criminals and wrong-doers in this way, I really wonder! After this incident, my attitude towards the accused persons underwent drastic change. I started thinking that the real incident of the accused person might not have been just the same, and that the accusation might be based on the wrong perception of the victim, too; it is quite possible.

In my life, thereafter, too, I have come across myriads of such incidents where without my mistake, the other party perceived me as guilty and quarrelled with me. How the principle of cause and effect works, I am not sure! Unless some

other domain is associated to the visible and perceptible realm!

The pioneering theft! I had lost my claim to get heaven after death, first of all, for no thief or scoundrel ever enters heaven, or the abodes of gods! Forsaking of Elysium for the sake of a petty pot of glass – an inkpot! Out of foolery! Without even any intention to steal! Simply with an intention to have fun I had done that prohibited act, and got thrown out of paradise – Paradise Lost! For me! Life is a very complex riddle! Unless one can be sure that one can swim across the turbulent torrents of an incident one should not venture to do any act; least of all a prank or a fun. Possibly this is the episode that prompted me very intensively in my heart to determine not to indulge in any act of stealing ever in future. I wrung my ears, as they did in our rustic area when they punished a culprit, and exclaimed to myself, '*Eh*, the sham hermit of innocent *Vedoo!* Do now become really as one *Vedoo* had thought me to be alike!'

XXX
Table of Contents

13. *Realm Of Decimal Points*
Enter Protagonist

In the process of speeding time and changing seasons coupled with the ever excruciating tantrums of my father at home – we never liked our father's presence at home, we always desired that he should not come home, he was a sure-shot source of ill-will and disquietude in the household. I was able to pass both the years of grade-3, the one which I attended first without regular admission in the school and the other one when I was admitted to school as a regular student yet retained in the third grade only, and that despite my being the crown student of the school. This was mourned for long, since in the process, my classmates had gone ahead leaving me behind. But there was one advantage of this retention: I was the brightest boy in the class without any challenger.

We had seen the realm of alphabets; we had seen the magic and mystery of numbers and arithmetic; we had relished as well as cherished the nectar of stories told by our favourite teacher – who got transferred elsewhere due to this alleged bad practice on his part – of story-telling to kids! We thought, we had nothing more to see as far as education or schooling was concerned. Nonetheless, in a wilderness, one can never be certain about anything! Thus far we had known only the Integers, that is, complete numbers, like one, two, ten, hundred etc. Of a sudden, one day our teacher – who had joined the school anew – entered our class; we were given to understand through grapevine that this particular teacher was a prodigy,

especially, of mathematics. We got elated to see the prodigy in our class. He was a lean and lanky yet energetic personality. His demeanour was affable, and he looked kind by his countenance and features.

He taught us about 'Decimal' points! Now, what is this new beast of this wilderness of literacy? Thought we small kids! The teacher told us that we might have seen certain numbers written with a point inserted in between them somewhere; and he gave an example by writing it by chalk on the black board. 'Black Board' used to be a proper noun those days for students and an omnipresent gadget or a ubiquitous apparatus of the school establishment! And the students used to have only wooden plaques to write on with the quills of reed dipped in *khadiyaa*, the liquid chalk or calcium.

He gave us the example of *Rupee* and its progeny – the *Paise*. Everybody in the class – 4th – knew that a *Rupee* consisted of one hundred *Paise! Rupee* and *Paise* were such a ubiquitous phenomenon! Rather, a predominant aspect of life's drama! Although most of the people know its significance in the drama of life, majority of them do not accord that much importance to this prominent aspect of life, particularly, social life, as is warranted, to live a decent and peaceful life! Most of the living beings – and human species is the only such creature – do not realise the primacy of monetary as well as financial aspect of life; they instead accord preponderant importance to the procreative aspect of life: to marriage and begetting of issues, the more the better in their perspective! And they suffer! Insufferably! Ironically, these carnal bodies consider only themselves having been assigned the crucial task of keeping the 'living' machinery of the Creation going by providing the requisite fodder in the form of babies consistently, yet they do not assume the pious duty of arranging Food, Shelter and Clothing for these begotten masses indispensably susceptible to all these requirements! They presume that the latter part is the sole responsibility of the Creator! To beget the children is the responsibility of man; to provide food, shelter and clothing that of the Creator! Queer logic of crazy as well as indolent souls! And they replace the Creator with society or the Govt, too, mostly when they find the Creator untraceable anywhere despite their sincere efforts to seek Him! In such circumstances, the Govt and the society become soft targets and can be bartered cheap! And blamed harmlessly!

Incidentally, the society never comes to the rescue of any beleaguered soul; it rather would dump one in gutter if given the choice. Society, of course, feigns to take care of those who are already well off, or well taken care of, and do not need any assistance from society.

The example of *rupee* and coins given by our Maths, or Arithmetic, teacher was perfect and thought-provoking for kids like me whose condition was miserable and wretched at home. The teacher also told us that the father and mother were the numbers written on the left side of the point sign and their issues were the numbers written to the right side of the point. To our laughter and amusement – us little kids! Such was his style of teaching; he was not famous for nothing! We did realise. Then he clarified – when we had laughed it out – that this smallest sign – the point – was called the 'Decimal Point'.

"What is it called?", sonorously sounded the affable teacher.

"The Decimal Point!", in chorus came the loud response from all the children.

"If the numbers to the left are there, the number to the left of decimal point is pronounced as absolute numbers, for example, such and such hundreds, such and such tens, such and such ones etc. And how are the numbers written to the right pronounced?", asked the teacher once again.

The teacher had in fact written a number with decimal point and the kids were asked to read that number. As was their wont, they read the digits to the right, too, as an absolute number like such and such hundred, such and such tens and such and such ones. That was the crux of the problem: of teaching.

"You are right to the left, yet wrong to the right!" he laughed heartily at this linguistic jugglery and went on to clarify, "You are incorrect so far as the digits written on the right side are concerned!" Thereafter, he went into a pause mode for quite a longwhile. The children kept peeking into his face – however, contorted comically, just like a cartoon, a caricature.

Then he exploded quite melodramatically, "The digits to the right would be called one by one individually, not as a joint combination of numbers!" And he enacted the reading for our comprehension.

This was a *de facto* sesame for us, for me, especially. So far, I had been knowing the numbers by their positions as hundreds, tens and ones; all of a sudden, the teacher had turned the tables on us as though; and declared that the rule that applied to the left of the decimal point did not apply to the right of the point. Strange! Why two norms to the same set of digits? Yet the rule is

rule, however, bizarre and unreasonable it might sound. The teacher also imbued in us the feeling that some people, even teachers, read it as absolute numbers and that the other method was incorrect.

Ever since then, I have never faltered in calling the digits to the right side of the decimal point individually and disparately. And that is easier as well; no straining of brains to decide whether the number we were going to call started with hundreds or thousands or millions or billions! Just calling single digits at a time individually!

Later on, in our adult life, we saw multitudes of educated and gifted persons of all hues reading the decimal numbers incorrectly, in absolute terms; and I always called to my mind my school teacher with reverence. It's only the teacher who can pass on the correct notions and pronunciations to the next generation. If teacher himself is ignorant, the entire edifice of learning might crumble. Unfortunately, that is what is happening post-colonial era, post the exodus of Britishers. In the zeal of bringing about social justice or so, all sorts of inefficiencies and deficiencies are being allowed to creep in to the schooling of children at the hands of unworthy and unlettered teachers!

God save the kids! Not only the king!

XXX
Table of Contents

11. Hesitation & Lost Innovative Potential

Enter Protagonist

We were assembled in the open space inside our school compound and our teacher – *Bhaagadbhoot* - was in fact taking the class. It seems to be very easy to take the class of children, yet in fact it is the toughest job of the conscious world: to teach the child or the children. Our teacher was making us children read a lesson from the *Hindee* text book turn by turn. That was a good practice: it gave the child the confidence to speak in front of a group, and also, tested his reading prowess and the knowledge of correct pronunciations, whether he could pronounce the words correctly or not. Albeit, *Hindee* is a phonetic language and there must be no confusion as regards pronunciation, yet there are many alphabets which can be pronounced in multiple manners; also, there are many words which over the time have undergone changes and, in turn, create confusions galore. Everybody claims that his pronunciation is standard, and also, that all others are in the wrong as regards pronunciation. When I was a child, and even now when I have come of age, I have not been able to solve this puzzle of 'which is correct or which is incorrect' as regards pronunciation of a letter or a word.

The matter of fact is that there is no such thing as correct or incorrect in this behalf: whatever has been in vogue over the time is considered as standard. And whatever goes beyond that boundary ignoring superstition is dubbed as incorrect. The same applies to spellings, particularly, in English! In English, in fact, the pronunciation is in a great mess! Unless heard from somebody, a word cannot be pronounced 'correctly' or, so to say, in the conventional manner, however, phonetically correct one might be. This sort of anomaly might have crept in the arena of language due to the eventual illiteracy of rulers – the kings or queens, the monarchs, emperors, or empresses etc. – whom, if they wrote or spelt or pronounced a thing incorrectly, nobody however gifted and correct one might be, could dare correct and tell that he or she – the ruler -- had spelled or pronounced the word incorrectly; who would! Who would like to be beheaded for the sake of merely being 'correct'! And that 'incorrect' thing would become the standard thing for good, for posterity. That's why all the mess in respect of English spellings and pronunciation! Still, however, nonsensical a tongue might be, if that is the tongue of a sovereign and the ruler, that is considered to be the superiest language in the world. By that token, the notions of superiority and inferiority are nothing but the outcomes of power plays.

Our teacher was a puritan and a person of old school, old thoughts; he was a stickler to correct pronunciations. When the students were reading the text, he was consistently as well as assiduously pointing out their mistakes and correcting their pronunciations as well as intonations. He was also clarifying the meaning of the words used in the lesson or the chapter. And we were relishing the session, even as, the season and weather were salubrious and we were seated in the open, in a pleasant breeze; and although normally of a strict mien, the teacher was kind towards children at that particular moment; we wondered what good thing had happened at his home front!

One such word used in the lesson was 'Dhaatu': 'Dhaatu ke bartan...' etc. By connotation its meaning was clear – the metal wares. The teacher asked the boy reading, "You know, what is the meaning of *dhaatu*?"

The boy could not tell. I knew the implied sense of the word *dhaatu* by way of its use in the sentence, but I did not have the exact wording for expressing its meaning. Given the opportunity I could have explained by example

that *dhaatu* was something like iron and aluminium etc. I longed to stand up and earn the kudos of the teacher but I could not gather courage due to my hesitation. The teacher asked everybody, nobody could tell. He, however, did not ask me. In the meantime, he explained exactly as I had surmised, by giving merely the example of iron, aluminium etc. made of which the utensils or wares in our households were. I lamented not having availed the wonderful opportunity to give further shine to my glory in the school. Hesitation hides many a great truth and fact, even the glow of wisdom! The wisest idea normally remains unspoken: due to the hesitancy and inexplicable inhibition of the thinker. Conversely, a vocal person might possibly be a shallow thinker!

Nonetheless, in the process, I could realise a greater phenomenon: that even if nobody answers and keeps mum, it does not necessarily imply that nobody knows; there might be many who were in the know but could not utter due to their lack of courage to speak in the group, or in front of the teacher, or due to paucity of proper words. How much truth thus might be remaining unexpressed, suppressed under the cloak of hesitation, lack of nerves, and also, due to fear and, at times, even under coercion of bullies and mafiosi!

I kept on lamenting this loss

of opportunity throughout my student life, yet could never embolden my nerves enough to speak up before the idiots, scoundrels or in public. I also realised that there might be some other kids as well like me who might be knowing the answer, or at least having the notion of what 'dhaatu' implied, yet due to weak nerves could not utter, since as soon as the teacher explained the meaning, many heads nodded and many faces glittered with enthusiasm, "Yes. Yes! I was thinking likewise!" I was also one amongst them: merely one amongst the melee!

I think, the most crucial issue of educating the children is to make them confident and communicative and rid them of their inhibitions in speaking before others whatever they might be thinking. Many a marvellous idea goes waste in this process of keeping reticent or remaining hesitant. Unfortunately, in the world, and in our country particularly, the opposite is practised: the kids are made to sit silently, and commanded rather 'not to speak nonsense', whereas in actuality the nonsense talk is the most sensible and most creative talk, given the state of affairs in human world, the society. Whatever is conventional is rotten and irrational as well as tyrannical!

XXX

Table of Contents

15. Well Head, Spring and the Koel

Enter Protagonist

Life offers umpteen number of incidents that etch in the grooves of brain for good. One such incident revolves around the well-head of a well obtaining inside our *Aadarsh Paathshaalaa* in town. During the winter season, particularly, our schools adopt the style of *Shaanti Niketan a la Gurudeva's* concept of teaching the children in the open, beneath the shade of vegetation; they – that is, teachers – had the liberty to take the children to the open space in the sunshine: of course, to ward off the chill that would be permeating the atmosphere within the four walls of the not-so-good rooms of the shop of education, the school, that is. And that change of atmosphere did wonders to the psyche of the little souls; they felt enthused to study and felt more vigorous outside than when they were kept indoors, within four walls, gloomy, that is.

On one such afternoon – and afternoons in winter season are always very short – our class was commanded to perch around the well-head of the well that was obtaining inside our school precincts. Well-head was safe for the children insofar as it had a sufficiently high boundary around it, that is, towards the well; there was thus no risk of kids plunging into the well inadvertently. That might have been the reason why our teachers oftentimes allowed the students of senior classes to use that patch of sunshine – around the well-head, particularly in the afternoon. Smaller ones, however, were still not allowed, may be due to their abnormal level of curiosity coupled with ignorance about the risks involved in satisfying that curiosity of peeking into the bottom of the well.

Sense of Risk is a very crucial trait that must needs to be imbibed in the brainy grooves of human beings lest the ignorant kids – why only kids, even grown-ups – should harm themselves inexorably, incorrigibly, irreparably. One such risk is ever present around the well-heads. Around that well-head, whenever our class used to be made to sit for taking lessons, I always felt a fear-psychosis inasmuch as I had already had my skull cracked in younger age by falling from the well-head of our family well. Yet, I noticed that my classmates of grade four couldn't help sneaking into the deep well from above the boundary of the well-head. I oftentimes cautioned them about the risks involved in their adventures but to only the derision of the mates who thought that I was being precocious. Despite the fact that I even used to show them the obvious scar on my skull! Whatever might be their

notions, but that was my reality! My experience! The others had not had chance to face that mishap. God forbid!

Nevertheless, this sitting around the well-head filled us with a sense of seniority inasmuch as we felt vividly that by sheer fact that we were allowed to perch there was proof enough that we were senior enough, and by implication had come of age – responsible age, at that. For, risk-taking may be allowed to only the sensible chaps!

We also felt that around the well-head, we were more efficacious inasmuch as we studied our lessons more energetically there.

In such a scenario, even as, it was a salubrious weather, my friend – the same friend who had misled me to the lathe-man earlier – induced me to bunk the class since the teacher was not there and normally the teacher seldom came to this spot after instructing the students to go sit around the well-head. We felt that nothing special was being achieved during those sessions except that we enjoyed the sunshine and felt relaxed, coupled with a sense of freedom. On the tree nearby, in fact, a *koel* had cooed and its song had inspired my chum to bunk the class.

We decided to hear the song of the *koel* for, after cooing for a short while at our nearby tree, it flew away, more so, because of the derision and pranks being played by children in the form of emulating its voice and song. The *koel* felt humiliated and chose to fly away from the buffoons that the little human kids were. We thought that we could follow the bird wherever it went. The area around the school was an open expanse unlike present day dense markets and residences. It used to be all trees, bushes, greenery and vegetation all around. Our *Paathshaalaa* itself looked as if it was outside the town, at an arm's length as though from the bustle of the business centre, the mart! Therefore, it was to some extent plausible to follow the *koel,* for it would fly from one tree to the other one, only thereabout, we presumed in our mind and left the class. We were three or four children I call to my mind presently.

The *koel* was cooing on the nearby tree only and we reached there and started mocking her song again. For a while we enjoyed the sonorous sound and song, yet the astute bird might have realised that some urchins were following her without the patent rights for singing, on which only the *koel* had the providential copyright; and it flew away, to our dismay again.

In our zeal, we reached another spot too where it had perched. In the process, in fact, we had gone quite far away from our school. Again, being an acknowledged intelligent student of the class, I started feeling pangs of anxiety concerning our teacher if he came to know of the fact that we were in the market during the school time. Chasing an innocent and unwilling *koel!* I asked my friends to return but they were absorbed in the pursuit of *koel* as if they were themselves some flying entities. I could not realise how a creature of land could dare suppose that one could follow a creature of air, both being the creatures of disparate domains. But the kids kept on pursuing the *koel.* At some distance they could trace a *koel* but it was some other *koel,* not the one they were pursuing thus far for its song.

They disputed for a while whether it was the same *koel* or some other one. I wondered what difference did it make whether it was the same *koel* or bird or some other one. It was singing, too! Moreover, all the *koels* looked alike; it was improbable for human beings to differentiate between two *koels*: which one was the first one that we were in pursuit of, was impossible to discern and decide.

Nevertheless, my chums disputed my contention by offering a bizarre rationale: they said that as all the girls could not be the same and that if someone was pursuing and courting a particular girl, it might not be that at some other spot he would start flirting with some other girl thinking that all girls looked alike; they don't look alike although!

"But *koels* look alike! To human eyes! *Koels* might be having the faculty for differentiating one *koel* from another one!", I proffered, but my mates didn't budge; they were intent on enjoying the spring season and its vocal feat, the *Koel.*

How it was that the black bird, not so cool to look at, came to fascinate all of us suddenly? It was because we had a poem entitled '*Koel*' in our fourth grade text-book and we had reached that lesson already, some of the lines of which were as follows:

Kaalee kaalee koo koo kartee,
Jo hai daalee daalee firtee,
Chhipee hare patton mein baithee ...

And this poem described our environs perfectly well: there was greenery, there was *koel* that was singing, and also, it was flapping from one branch to another one as well as to other trees.

After a while, the *koel* thought it fit to fly away beyond the sight of us flirtatious two-legged lovers. We saw it vividly cruising towards the horizon; we could not help returning in that situation to our roost – the school. Dejected! Yet, we were reciting our poem, imagining in our mind's eye the same *koel* as per our sweet will.

XXX

Table of Contents

16. First Feelings Of Romance

Enter Protagonist

I was a shy guy, a self-conscious chap, hesitant to talk to female species, the girls! I knew very well that there were two types of human beings: male and female; that it's not a unitary entity, the human species: it's dichotomic. I was too much female-conscious in fact from the beginning, from my birth itself. From the very infancy, my caretakers or whosoever were bringing me up, made me over conscious about the speciality or attractiveness of female folks; for instance, they would say, "You will get a wife, a beautiful wife!", even though I did not know what 'beautiful' was and what 'wife' implied. Of course, on one stray occasion I had already been made to act as the child bridegroom for one lady, the wife of my mother's cousin in our *Nanihaal.* From that moment, I had somehow harboured a notion that the particular lady was my half-wife, albeit only notionally, even though I could not do anything about it except surmising that I was already a groom of a grown-up lady.

That was not the only instance: my mother was a jolly natured lady and loved to behave romantically and erotically. In fact in her father's village, they were quite prosperous people and had no monetary problems. When one does not have any problems and sorrows

– especially, monetary --, one tends towards either sensual pleasures or towards intoxicants. We have observed after having come of age that these two recourses are taken even when one is over worried and wretched, that is, just the opposite extreme of earlier conditions. Both the ends of the spectrum lead to the same seemingly pleasurable pastures of sensuality, dissipation and intoxication. My mother oftentimes used to remark, whenever I was sighted playing with some girl of my age, that she would marry me with her. This intonation gradually carved inside me a special consciousness, a special sensitivity, towards womenfolk inasmuch as I thought that all those girls would one day be eligible to become my wives and my source of sensual pleasures. Before time, in this process, I became precocious, utterly hypersensitive, so to say towards opposite sex.

The result was that I never felt at ease in the presence of even girl babies and girl children. Whenever I came in their company, whilst other children behaved quite normally and could play with them and mix up with them without getting self-conscious, I was the crazy one who felt awkward and restive, and immediately tended to blush, becoming self-conscious, and could not muster courage to play with them or to talk to them. This

was a very embarrassing situation for me as well. I disliked my psyche, the trait of over consciousness towards the fair sex, but could do nothing about it. Because I was being told that every girl was related to me: sensually, maritally in long run! Long run or short run, the psyche had captured that run and started getting fascinated or infatuated by that phenomenon. Nonetheless, I observed that the girls did not feel any such feeling towards me, for they were not imbibed with that feeling: they were not intoned that every boy was a potential husband for them. That sort of self-consciousness did me great harm in forming my personality when I grew up, also, even when I was merely a child or an adolescent.

Because I did not know what sensuality was, what beauty implied, what the use of these attributes was, what the use of women was in one's life, I developed a sense of fear from the side of female sex. I dreaded girls. Not only girls, I was shy of dealing with or conversing with even the grown-up ladies. And that made me look like a fool and a damned bore in the society. A boredom! A *Bodum!* In colloquial parlance.

One such awkward equation, for instance, was in relation to the wife of our maternal cousin in whose marriage party we had gone by bullock cart merely as toddlers. She was decades or more older than I was, yet I felt shy while dealing with her; I never talked to her, nor did I ever address her by any appellation; I felt as if that was an anathema for me to speak to a lady, as if my mere talking would foul the thin line of chastity between me and the adult lady. I behaved like an adult at psychic level. One of the factors of this awkward behaviour on my part towards the householder as well as familial lady was that she was very pretty and I could not help becoming self-conscious in the presence of a pretty woman or girl even as a child. It made me abnormally self-conscious and awkward. For this abnormal behaviour of mine I was oftentimes chastised too, even by my mother, not only by others. But it was none of my fault. My impressionable child's psyche had been defiled inexorably by the elders themselves. Or maybe I was a lascivious person, a *zameendaar* or a feudal lord in my previous birth, the *sanskaars* of which had been transmitted hither, to this birth. And that possibility could not be ruled out outright, for I was born not further from the period of abolition of feudal and princely system. After dying from there I would have been born here, endowed with the same consciousness on subconscious level.

Not many girls fortunately were in our school, or in our class. Incidentally, not many people were still comfortable with sending their daughters and sisters to schools: a hangover of the *Muslim* era. But whatever girls – one or two – were there in our school or in our class, were enough to arouse my awkward feeling. I evaded their company, even evaded conversing with them, and even evaded seeing towards them. It was such a bizarre disease, psychic one! I in fact felt tormented in their presence.

Outwardly demeanour is no guarantee that one would be behaving similarly psychically as well. The more abstinence I observed outwardly, the more sensuous feeling I felt inwardly towards the females, although I vowed that I would have nothing to do with womenfolk, that I would not marry anybody, that I would live a life of celibacy throughout. I was fascinated by the tales of *Brahmachaarees*, by the biography of *Swaamee Dayaanand*, and other like sages. I could not even think in my wildest dreams that I would ever have to do anything with girls or women.

Nonetheless, for I avoided them, they became the inescapable point of attention for me. Allegorically, the tale of a saint and his devotee: wherein the saint suggested the *chelaa* (disciple) as remedy the process doing which the latter had not to remember a monkey or monkeys, lest the remedy would go waste. And by remedy itself it was bound to fail: remembrance is such a paradoxical phenomenon! Whomsoever one wants to forget does necessarily come to mind first of all! Unless I saw them – the female folk -- I did feel depressed. As soon as I sighted my classmates – girls - without even seeing towards them I felt enthused, a thrill in my chest and spine. The abstinence and resolve was in fact acting in reverse direction. I was a child, how could I help it!

There was one girl from our village who attended our school, I think, our class. Whenever I sighted her I felt special feelings aroused in my heart. She hailed from a very wealthy family, and my father had good relations with that family. Without even having any connections with her or without being on talking terms with her, I needed her presence in the class or school for arousing my enthusiasm towards studies and for boosting my intelligence up. Queer feeling!

I normally used to accompany my mates from and to school but I felt that I could move faster – rather at a trot like a horse, a stallion – and could reach the village far ahead of other mates. I decided to adopt my gait – a horse's trot – which accelerated my speed as if I were flying on some avionics. This was yet another unique experience and discovery of mine, for myself.

One day I started walking like this and from that day the playmates started calling me a horse, a stallion, in that I trotted like a horse. But I liked that horse-power of mine. I used to leave the whole group far behind me and used to travel all alone relishing my new invention in the arena of velocity and acceleration. My ladylove or lady Friday, if one likes to name it like that, one day hailed me from behind, I don't know, for what purpose – she was in the group of boys – and I blushed at merely this innocuous calling by a little girl, feeling abashed to have been called by her like this in front of other boys. I felt in my childish supposition that the other boys would take it otherwise, that a young girl was talking to a boy, and that they would make fun of me. I was the brightest boy of the school and class, and this gift might have tempted the pretty girl to be attracted towards talking to me. I felt a thrill but could not muster courage enough to converse with her. She tried to catch up with me but with my newfound way of trotting like a horse, or a colt, I kept ahead and she could not catch up with me. I was sure about that: nobody could catch up with me, neither in speed, nor in mental acumen, the academic performance, that is.

In academics, I had devised a tool to leave everybody behind and climbed the pinnacle of glory; now in speed, I had devised a style whereby I could leave everybody behind me in physical world. I felt myself on the seventh sky for my two divine gifts of brightness and velocity!

Nothing though unusual happened in respect of my relations with that pretty girl from my village and acquaintances, yet I kept on feeling a thrill in my heart all along whenever I sighted her or felt her presence around. I could never define that feeling in any terms: that was certainly not sensual, nor romantic, nor erotic. Merely a fascination towards an opposite sex, fair sex, about whose pleasures my mother and acquaintances had fed my subconscious mind so much without my grasping the import of that!

That was my first feeling of, if you may call it, Love or Romance! A fool's romance!

XXX

Table of Contents

17. Language Teacher & Pronunciations

Enter Protagonist

On the one hand, there was this undefined as well as unfathomable titillating undercurrent of romance and fascination towards the fair sex, on the other hand, we heard about one of our teacher's estrangement with his wife. He was our favourite teacher; he taught us language. His conception of teaching was very intelligible and impressive. We revered this young teacher; he was younger in the group of teachers in our school. He was a bit drab, dry and cold, no doubt, but he never flogged or rebuked any child.

One day he was exceptionally morose and in a dejected mood. He put up the mobile wooden black board on a trellis and started writing some words with the chalk on it. He wrote their meanings against them. He also pronounced those words in his unique style. It was he only who taught us the correct pronunciations of vowels of *Hindee* alphabet. Thus far we pronounced some of the alphabets and the words wrongly: in fact in our colloquial style as we spoke in our village.

When our revered teacher pronounced '*Kaii*' we children smiled and were startled and thought that he was pronouncing it like that for fun's sake, to make us kids laugh. But that was not his wont. I think I or someone else dared to ask, too, "*Maassaab*, it is pronounced as *Kaiee*!"

He did not get angry; he was well aware that throughout the

area, and even in the town, all and sundry were pronouncing this word like that only -- *Kaiee*. He, therefore, clarified that correct pronunciation of the word was as he was pronouncing, and that whatever the people pronounced was not correct, given the nuances of *Hindee* language, particularly *Devanaagaree* script. He also corrected us in respect of many other letters, particularly, '*Jna*', which we and everybody pronounced as '*Gya*'. He pronounced it for us and it was clear that it was not *Gya*, however, in between *Jna* and *Gya*. For simplicity's sake, the convention took it as Gya and now that is in vogue, *Jna* having been dropped, its grammatical and etymological superiority notwithstanding. This shows how convention prevails upon dry truth and eventually shrouds it!

Further, he clarified one more alphabet though he told us that we children needed not stretch our minds that much for that was beyond the pale of our realm. He expounded it and pronounced the composite letter '*Sra*' as in '*Sahasra*' and clarified that many people pronounced it as '*Stra*' as in '*Stree*', and pronounced as '*Sahastra*' which is wrong. Nuanced pronunciations of '*Dya*' and '*Dma*' as in '*Vidyaa*' and '*Padma*' which some ignoramuses pronounced as '*Viddhaa*' and '*Padya*' etc. That

session proved to be revealing for us kids. Now that revelation set me on the train of thinking that unless these sounds were heard from the mouth of someone, an exponent of language, how could one grasp their correct pronunciation, however, skulduggery one might indulge in! That is why language may be learnt only by listening; merely by reading from the book one cannot grasp the correct or conventional pronunciation. *Vidyaa* is, therefore, said to be closely associated with voice, the sound and, in turn, *Guru.*

That is where the significance of good teacher comes into picture. If the teacher himself or herself is unaware of the correct nature of the language, entire edifice of pious temple of language would come crashing down. Unfortunately, it is exactly this what is happening these days. In the zeal to bring about social justice by means of reservations to lower and weaker sections of society, the purity and integrity of language and education is being compromised. I am afraid, a day is not far off when students would be taught '*Ga*' for '*Ka*' and '*Gha*' for '*Kha*'! Who will decide then what is right or what is wrong! Amongst the judges if there were dispute, who would decide what is right or what is wrong. Depending merely on majority view is a misleading concept inasmuch as if majority of the people are duffers, they would give the judgement simply verging on foolishness!

Our teacher was so bright and pure in respect of language; his teachers, in turn, would have been puritans and might have taken pains to keep the language and pronunciation pristinely pure. It goes to suggest that the condition of education was intact even during the British era or *Muslim* era; it's only after what they call 'Independence' that all the chaos has broken out and has dismantled the temple of education irreparably, as though. People are passing out of schools and colleges, yet they may be perfectly unlettered and uneducated, however paradoxically. The educational degrees and certificates have become inconsequential! Of little value, of course!

No child amongst us, nevertheless, had the courage to ask the teacher whether what we had heard about his estrangement with his wife was correct. Nonetheless, everybody was sympathetic towards our beloved teacher, even without expressing it.

I for my part set off musing that even such a pleasurable entity as wife, that is formed of female folk, fair sex, in whose praise so much is made out by my mother and her acquaintances in front of me, and I am associated with them from my babyhood itself, could turn out to be a phenomenon abominable!

For our beloved teacher!

Later on, we were given to understand by one of our mates who was more inquisitive as well as resourceful than we were that it was not due to any defect in the female qualities of the fair sex but due to difference of opinion in respect of their dealings with their parents, that is, the in-laws of the wife of our teacher. He had taken the side of his parents; those were aged couple. And as usual, the wife wanted to get rid of those old skulls who 'were past sanity and had already turned senile'.

I thought that there were thorns in every flower of roses and in most of the flowers! My resolve to never get entangled with any girl or later with any lady got firmed up more and more. Nonetheless, I kept on feeling excited at the sight of any fair sex without exception, which I could not help ever even thereafter.

XXX

Table of Contents

18. The Tongues Of The Unlettered

Enter a Class-Mate

We were classmates and we were friends, too. Fast friends, that is. I hailed, however, from a caste which was considered lower and my friend was from a caste which was considered upper. The only difference that we could discern between our families and their status was that we lived in congested and smaller habitats mostly made from *kutcha* soil or bricks and my friend had his habitat in a bigger compound of rooms that were constructed around a spacious plot of land. Nonetheless, I could see that the personal living space of the family my friend could claim to be their own was only half a room, rather, one-third of a long *kutcha* room. By that token, we were far better; they had no private place of their own. Theirs was a joint family, a feudal set-up: everything straitjacketed. Being of the so-called lower class we and our female folks had sufficient liberty to move around and work physically outdoors in the fields whereas they and their ladies could not venture out and could not think of working with their hands physically; their domain was restricted to only that compound and in that too only within that half or third of a shared room. How claustrophobic and suffocating that atmosphere might be, can only be surmised. Even for nature's call they could go to the fields only at night suffering throughout the day.

I had been to their habitats whenever I got ready for school before my friend could and he was somewhat late in coming to my residence, if you can call it. I never felt at ease when there in their habitats waiting for my friend. His father was a person whose eyebrows were always warped and drawn, for what reason I could never fathom; he was never seen speaking affably with anybody, least of all with the babies and children. This was the typical characteristic of feudal system that therein the male folks considered themselves as Almighty and immortal, never to die or lick the dust in life. Arrogance was their primary jewel and embellishment; the more scoundrel a feudal male the better and upper his caste was considered to be. They were rascals I knew it well, even as, my parents exhorted me likewise, and also, our text-books preached accordingly. Nowhere we could feel that arrogance, the pride of caste and class; the showing off of pelf and financial status of a person were the signs of superiority of a human being.

In fact, our family vocation was to cut the hair of the village folks, that is, hair dressing in contemporary parlance, if you would like to name it that way. We were also vested with the unwritten authority and privilege to settle the marriages of lads and lasses from variegated villages, for it were we only who used to travel the distance between various places and to accomplish the tasks assigned; the upper caste people could neither go there nor was it in vogue that one party could see the would-be bride or bride-groom in advance. It used to be a game of chances! A gambling! A groping in the dark! Perfect dark!

We were friends because I was a brilliant boy of the school and class thus far, and now a new prodigy had sprung up amazingly in the form of my young friend, and we thought it expedient to make friends with each other. The wavelengths of same type resonate with their likes! We used to traverse the distance between our village and the town together; and we prided in that. Our temperaments were alike, too, both of us being of gentle and polite mien and having chastity as our traits. We liked to behave in a decent and civilized manner, unlike that of vulgar chaps who attended the school, too, yet behaved like rustic urchins on the way. We never did. Our parents used to preach us all sorts of pious things including, "Always speak the truth!" and my mother had preached me that this single precept was enough to follow in one's life, also, that no other education was warranted apart from this pursuit. I had followed my mother's instructions literally and always tried to speak the truth. My friend oftentimes was bemused at my cynicism, for he contended that it was almost improbable to stick to truth perfectly, that the circumstances of life and society were such that one had voluntarily or involuntarily to resort to lies so as to survive. My friend contended that to decide as to what was true, that is, real, and what was false, that is, hypocritic, was quite impossible inasmuch as it all depended upon one's value system and circumstances of upbringing. A thief would never consider the theft as a misdeed lest he should give up stealing and starve to death; likewise a rapist or sexual wrong-doer never considers it as a foul play lest one should rid oneself of that depravity.

I told my friend that I was trying to stick to truth to the maximum of my abilities and that, well, I too told lies sometimes. My friend was very much impressed by my good and imitable demeanour, although he never claimed that he would pursue only the path of truth.

One day, when he was at my habitat, as I was late in getting ready for the school, he saw many a picture hung on the *kutcha* walls of our room. All were calendars showing pictures of religious tales, though not true, nor realistic, but the import of those pictures was noble: to induce the people to follow the path of righteousness. My mother was in the habit of expounding the themes of those pictures to whoever child happened to visit our home. Seeing my friend curiously watching the lovely pictures, my mother, an unlettered and uneducated lady even as she was, proceeded to explain the stories depicted in the pictures to my friend.

In one of the pictures, a ferocious black woman was standing with one foot on the body of a monstrous daemon lying on the floor. My mother explained that the woman with weapons in her hand was the goddess and the person lying on the floor was a '*Raakhas*'. At this, my friend enquired as to what *Raakhas* was, for in our books we had read about '*Raakshas*' but nowhere had we heard the term '*Raakhas*'. My mother tried to explain by enumerating the bad qualities of a *Raakhas*. My friend wanted to clarify whether the same was a *Raakshas*, but my mother being unaware of the nuances of language stuck to her guns that 'no, it was not *Raakshas*, it was *Raakhas*'. I did also not know, and my friend also could not discern the difference between a *Raakhas* and a *Raakshas*.

When we left the home for school, on the way, we were discoursing on the topic of *Raakhas*. In no way we were able to make out that the mother was pronouncing the same thing in her unlettered tongue and could not know the lettered word. It was only after many days that my friend told me, "Your mother might be telling us about *Raakshas* and was calling it *Raakhas*." How could I go against my mother's version; I stuck to her guns saying that *Raakshas* was

entirely different from a *Raakhas*.

Those were the days of spring season, rather, harvesting season. The village people were busy handling the ripened crops. On the way, we used to observe that grains were strewn all around having fallen from the carts that had carried them. I used to lament the loss of so much quantity of grains this way, for lot many grains were seen also strewn in the fields from which the harvest had been picked. My friend, however, was of the other opinion: he said that it was only these fallen grains that the creatures other than human beings fed upon, and that it was their share of the food grains; also, that the poor people might glean the fallen grains from the fields for their stomachs, for they did not have their own fields. It was such an inequitable social setup! It still is! This condition used to continue for about two months and thereafter everything changed, even the season changed, and the blizzards of summer season started and we found our schools closed, and sensibly so.

The seasoned elders of the past had already arranged well all the activities of human society based on empirical data and making the best of their experiences of season, weather, wind, sun and moon etc. over the millennia!

On another such day, my friend heard my mother say '*Tashak*

Taal' and he set on musing what this *Tashak Taal* could be, for he was now fully convinced that my mother was only saying the words in her unlettered tongue, not in the tongue of literate people. She was also right in her conviction insofar as there could be no birth right to decide what was wrong or what was right as regards nomenclature or pronunciation of words. People follow only the convention set by influential and powerful people. My friend was able to decipher this bizarre script as well; he told me after some days that what my mother meant to call by *'Tashak Taal'* was actually *'Takshak Taal'*. Of *Mahaabhaarata* repute!

"Wow! What a *Eureka!* You are a genius! You will certainly fill the chasm between the two tongues, that is, the unlettered and lettered ones," I exclaimed and burst out into loud laughter on the way to school, to my friend's bemusement and bewilderment.

XXX

Table of Contents

19. Schooling Savagery

Enter Father

In the millet field where we were weeding our undergrowth from the crop, after I had finished the story of my untimely marriage and resultant financial disaster I was stalked with, my son enquired abruptly, "Tell us something about your teaching life at the town school. Also, tell us about the episode wherein a teacher had been beaten by the students."

"How come you know about all that, I mean, about the manhandling of the teacher by students?"

"I was at that time in fourth standard at *Aadarsh Paathshaalaa.* One day, there was lot of buzz in the town, and also, in our school about the incident in that a teacher had been manhandled by students in the higher secondary school."

"What was the reaction of students? That is, in your school?" I enquired.

"The children were enthused as if some great revolution had taken place, as if it were some welcome step! This was something entirely unimaginable for those little souls: that a student or some students could gather courage to beat their teacher even. We were somehow pleased subconsciously: any act of subversion engenders lot of energy and euphoria amongst the masses, particularly, the innocent inexperienced youths. Something had been done that had shattered the established norms of society!" my son put forth his ideas.

He also added, "Yet another day, around the timing of the same episode, I had also heard one of the students of your school telling me that my father – that is, you -- had had a bout of cholera in the school;

and he expressed it so gleefully as if it were a happy augury for me. At which, I felt amazed how this scoundrel of a lad could derive satisfaction from the saddening news of my father's having been infected with cholera."

My son, however, did not divulge the fact that aside from being bewildered at the behaviour of the student, he would have also felt to some extent alike in that his father having had cholera was a good thing for them insofar as that way they – he and his mother – would have gotten rid of my tyranny. Human psychology works like that: finding oneself incapable to avenge anybody's tyranny, one draws perverse pleasure whenever one comes to know about the tyrant's agony. It makes little difference whether one is related to oneself or not.

I ventured to narrate my life-span at the town school thus:

"After having plucked in B. Ed. from *Ganj Dundwaaraa* – and I had failed in *Practicals*, you know, the teaching classes of the B. Ed. course, in which everybody normally qualifies...."

"Queer! There must have been something definitely fishy on your part about the whole training session otherwise there was no question of one failing in teaching classes, that too, in B. Ed., wherein so many good-for-nothing teachers abound all around due to lenient system of educational teaching training! And for a lad who had secured second division in his BA course, that too, in Arts stream! Not a small achievement! That prodigy was made to fail in a commonplace course like that of B. Ed.! Quite unfathomable!", interposed my sensible son.

"That's right! In fact, at *Ganj Dundwaaara*, I was staying with my cousin, the eldest son of my younger *Buaajee*. And you know, they were rich and influential landlords of their area. This cousin of mine was a totally spoiled brat of that feudal system; he had already disfigured his face in an almost fatal accident and his face looked now a deformed and horrid one, alike that of a fiend. Even the serious accident did not deter him from his depraved and dissipated life-style verging on arrogance, conceit, showing-off and intoxication."

"How can one think of pursuing one's studies staying with such a brat?", commented my son in disgust, adding, "You would as well have been equally arrogant and spoilt in the company of such a brat!"

"Yes, I too was equally spoilt a brat in his company."

"What was he there? I mean, how he was there at *Ganj Dundwaaraa*; and how it was that you found yourself there in his company, leaving aside all the good places of your area?", my son rightly asked.

"He was a scion of feudal set-up and they had influence in that area, and also, might be having influence in the Educational Training School there. My cousin got a job in Agriculture Deptt, for job in Agriculture sector was considered in those days to be the most coveted job, particularly in rural areas, and he was posted there. And my situation being fluid and miserable at that juncture, having squandered all the jewellery of my wife including the bangles of my son, I was in the bad and abhorrent habit of visiting my relatives quite frequently: from one relative to another and from another to the third one and so on; there were plenty of them those days and all were quite wealthy."

"Did you not feel ashamed to go to your relatives quite so often? For I had heard our elder uncle – *Mausaajee* – taking exception to this habit of yours, and making it a point of objection and complaint time and again, this habit of yours burdening by your presence the relatives' establishments quite so often. *Mausaajee* also added that those relatives did not take it kindly and did not like your visiting them so frequently and staying there for months together without any cause and purpose. Relatives are not meant

for burdening them with one's presence. Particularly, one must avoid burdening the houses of lady's in-laws," my son expressed with a sense of vexation and pique.

I felt hurt as was my wont; I could not stand any affront to my insolence. My brainwaves worked quite on different wavelength: I thought it quite usual to give trouble to my relatives again and again. After all, what are the relatives meant for? For entertaining the relatives only! However, I never could think in converse order: if those relatives happened to think likewise and offered to visit me quite so often, what would have been my condition? I lacked wherewithal of any sort whatsoever!

"While studying at *Ganj Dundwaaraa*, I had put on stake all the jewellery of my wife for pursuing the phony course of B. Ed. which was supposed to be the lynchpin of my future financial career. Notwithstanding such a great stake, I was foolish enough like *Yudhisthir* – of *Mahaabhaarata* repute who had put on stake his wife in gambling – to not caring seriously about my studies. I was under the false impression that my relatives being influential people passing the exam would be a cat-walk, rather, a walk-over for me. That did not come true!

"Most of my time there was spent not on the studies but on

loitering as well as loafing around along with my cousin and on boozing with him as well, almost on daily basis. We consumed drugs, too. We did care little for the Principal of the school. My Principal had had a tiff with my cousin and warned me against my having any truck with my cousin. How could I shun the company of my cousin: I was equally spoilt a brat at that time. I had the false notion that we were scions of great *khaandaans* (ancestries, pedigrees), contemplating little that notwithstanding that, our actual social and financial condition had nothing to sing home about; we were penniless at the material time.

"When it was time of exams, I could write the exams successfully and was still overconfident that I would qualify the exam. However, that was not to be! When the result came, I had failed; and not in written exam, but in Practicals: in the Teaching sessions. The antagonism of the Principal had cost me so dearly, so precious a degree as B.Ed.! Still, I was foolhardy enough to think that it mattered little and that despite not having a Teaching degree, the basic requirement for getting a teaching job, I would manage to get a teaching job at the town school; I had so much faith in the clout of my family and acquaintances – in the feudal system. Typically, that in

itself was a characteristic of the feudal system: not to have realisation about the ephemerality of everything including the time and space!

"At town school, however, *Bhaiyaajee* – my cousin who had his in-laws as great a family as the progenies of *Mahaaraajaa Chhatrasaal* from *Chhaataa Teekamgarh* state was the member of the Management of the school. In my short-sightedness, I took him as an omnipotent persona of the area, as if keeping him in good spirits would guarantee me a permanent job in the school notwithstanding my ineligibility and inability to complete the Teaching Training course. *Bhaiyaajee* was in fact in the *Management* of the school, for the founder and owner of the school – *Chaubeyjee* – was his friend from schooling days. The job I could get somehow both due to the influence of *Bhaiyaajee* and the goodwill of my pedigree." *Bhaiyaajee* himself was a spoilt brat, a bully, rather, and the grapevine had it that he was such a scoundrel that one day he rode his bicycle, reached the town, climbed the knoll of mud nearby – a relic of the habitations of the *Nawaab* of the town who had eventually fled to *Paakistaan* in the wake of partition – and riding the bicycle himself, let it go freely hurtling down the precarious slope of the knoll, and understandably hurt himself badly.

"Nonetheless, you were a graduate of that time, the only graduate of the area. Also, your father was an influential person having high connections with powerful persons in the Govt and Administration, why didn't you try to get any other job than this lack-a-daisical, rather ramshackle, *ad hoc* job of teaching?", interposed my son.

"It is not that I did not try to get a better job."

"Why didn't you take the competitions for jobs?", my son justly asked. I had no answer to this valid poser; I simply dodged this inquisition, for the fact is, I never could gather courage to take a competition. I had no such common sense. My mind could not think beyond the feudal clout of my family and acquaintances which could get me a job by dishonest means and contrivances. I could not think of climbing the ladder of financial self-sufficiency through the righteous route of fair competition, proving my worth and mettle. I didn't have that mettle as my son commented later on.

"My father sent me to his friends who were in high and mighty positions and had themselves the powers to appoint me, too. For instance, he sent me to one of his friends with his recommendations. When I approached one of such worthies, he received me with zeal, and enquired about my father, his school days' friend, enthusiastically. He assured me that he would get me a job when he heard that I was a graduate. He was writing the order for my posting when I kneeled on his table with my elbows on his desk. He looked at me with vexation and pique and stopped writing forthwith and ruefully remarked, "Oh, you do not know the manners how to stand in front of a higher official, you are quite unfit for the job."

"In yet another instance, my father sent me to yet another friend of his with his note of recommendation. He too received me with enthusiasm on learning that I had come from his school days' friend. He too agreed to give me a job and started writing my appointment letter when suddenly something struck his mind and he enquired of me whether I had 'Geography' as a subject in my High School. I denied. He nodded his head in dejection, "Oh, in our department, we take geography as a compulsory qualification. Sorry! Come another day!"

"In this way, I had been to many senior officials and all of them had asked me to come later on, some other day, and they assured me that they would give me a job somehow."

"Then, did you go to them later on, some other day, for getting the job, as they had demanded of you?" asked my son in a perplexed tone.

I had no answer and I evaded the question by showing myself busy in the weeding job at hand in the field. In fact, I had a deranged brain and it never struck my mind that I had been called by the officials to come some other day, and unless I went there again – some other day - how could I get a job! My son detected this flaw in my aptitude and remarked, "There had been a basic flaw in your common sense and approach towards getting a job. One, you never tried the Kingsway of competition. Second, you approached the influential friends of your father and they assured you to get a job and asked you simply to come on a later day but you never approached them later on; how could you then get a job? They were not supposed to come to you with a job on platter and offer you at your home."

I kept mum and became displeased with my son and expressed it too, "It is all due to fate-line! It all depends on one's fate!"

"Fate-line is nothing but lack of common-sense and enterprise on the part of the person!", remarked my son with bewilderment mixed with vexation. "Anyway, tell us about your teaching job at the town school; it seems you had decided in your mind to remain at your village and teach at school only", he added.

"I got a job easily at the town school; *Chaubeyjee* was under the awe of our family's pedigree. Also, *Bhaiyaajee* used his good offices in tilting the balance in my favour. Otherwise also, there were no competitors as regards teaching of English language those days, particularly, in our area.

"In that school, I was treated as a crown prince amongst the teachers. They had the impression that I hailed from some royal family; such was the goodwill and fame of our family and our ancestors! This status and treatment moved my head and my head had swollen too much."

"It was already swollen, nevertheless!", interjected my son sensibly.

"I was like a don amongst the teachers and I now realise that they started using me as an instrument of nuisance. To trouble the Principal, and in turn, the Management. They created a sham nuisance value for me."

"For instance? Nuisance value, what's that?" my son asked.

"For instance, they used me as a goon, a bully. To set right the other ones. Let me clarify. Many of us teachers smoked despite the injunction to the contrary by the school Principal and the

Management, that is, not to smoke in the school. But we – some of the teachers – used to smoke nonchalantly even in the school."

"Very bad! Really shameful!", remarked my son.

"There were some other teachers who did not smoke, and also, objected to the smoking in school. One such teacher was a very nice fellow and an apparently gifted one. He objected to some teachers smoking in the school. Our Principal was also against smoking in the school, but he was from some lower caste and had not the guts to forbid the teachers of so-called upper caste from smoking in the school. Therefore, he asked the teacher in question to forbid the smokers from smoking in the school. One day, in the Staff Room, he chastised the smoking teachers on this score.

"The teachers ganged up against the sane as well as sensible teacher, yet they had no clout or guts to oppose him. Their only hope was me. I was a smoker but I did not smoke in the Staff Room. The day the teacher had chastised the teachers I was not amongst them. The aggrieved gang of smokers approached me, for they thought that I was the most foolish brat in the school. They induced me to take on the sensible naysayer by smoking in front of him. I climbed the grapevine. I deliberately went to the chamber where the teacher was seated and started smoking there. He objected to, and that was exactly what I wanted, an excuse to start a squabble, a tussle. I told him articulately and rudely, "Nobody can stop us from smoking here! Stop us if you dare!"

"But that was very bad of you! What was the reaction of gentle and sensible teacher?", asked my son curiously with the lines of pain having emerged on his forehead.

"He became morose and asked in a dejected manner, 'We are trying to establish a good culture in the school but if people like you also try to spoil the atmosphere, what can we do! etc.'

"I felt as though I had won a big battle."

"Demoniac victory! A fiendish bravado!" remarked my son peevishly.

"Yes, now in hindsight I think so, too! After sometime the teacher left the school and went somewhere else, at a better post possibly."

"*Dhamma* helped him and punished you! In hindsight you can see vividly!", my son remarked. I felt humiliated at this deduction of my son and allusion to *Dhamma*.

"But the story of the manhandling of the teacher remains to be told as yet.", my son insisted.

"Well, from the side of our village, students of the nearby village – *Kapnaa* --normally met with me and accompanied me on the way to the school. In that village, there used to be a bully, a mafia, a muscleman, you know his name! Those boys were under my influence as ours was a much ferocious mafiosi. In fact, they were sort of urchins, spoilt boys. I myself being a spoilt boy liked their misdemeanour. Like-minded company of all the brats!

"In our school, it was the system of co-education, that is, both girls and boys studied together. Co-education is the root of all the evils in the society."

"How is co-education an evil? What harm is it doing to the society?", asked my son.

"You won't understand. It is breaking the caste system."

"You want caste system to be perpetuated?"

"Yes, caste system is the backbone of our culture."

"Not of culture, but of feudalism!", remarked my spoilt son sarcastically.

"Anyway, you won't understand. Coming to our teaching tales, there were girls also studying in the school. And there was this teacher who had been beaten. He was posted as a PT teacher. He was, however, seen as showing too much closeness towards the girl students and this trait of his was not liked by some of the teachers, like me, and also, by the students."

"Nonetheless, the girls were merely little children – High School students; what harm could be done to them? The sensible teacher would be showing paternalistic caressing attitude towards them as towards his own daughters and children."

"Maybe, but general impression was that his behaviour was beyond the boundaries of acceptable civil and moralistic behaviour."

"Nonetheless, how is it related to his manhandling at the hands of those students, the scoundrels?"

"Those few students told me one day on the way to school that that particular teacher was troubling them; that in PT class, he targeted them particularly and subjected them to physical punishment selectively, that this mistreatment of theirs had been continuing for quite a while. They asked me what they should have done. They also said that they felt like beating the teacher next time if he misbehaved and ventured to punish them."

"What did you suggest them?"

"What else could I have suggested? I suggested them that the next time if the teacher misbehaved with them and punished them, they should do as they liked!"

"But that's pretty savage! You did not talk to the teacher and counsel him sensibly?", my son was stupefied at my suggested course of action. However, I could not think anything sensible other than that. That was as per my mental build. If I could beat my wife heartlessly without any concern for hurts to her body, the mind and self-esteem, what was it for me to have a peer level teacher beaten at the hands of scoundrels. I was least concerned about its ramifications and social impacts.

"What by the way happened thereafter?"

"You know what happened thereafter. After a few days, the untoward incident took place: as the teacher proceeded to punish the boys, some of them slapped him in the face and manhandled him as the brutes normally do."

"Thereafter? Did the school faculty and Management suspect you?"

"They did. There was mayhem in the school, and also, in the entire area. The beaten teacher accused me of being in cahoots with the accused chaps. Naturally, I denied. They proposed to rusticate the students from the school and assigned the task to me which I denied to execute. That reinforced their suspicion on me. That's the tale of that untoward incident."

"That was very savage of you, no doubt!", my son sighed, "Your *kamma* has rightly caught up with you, now viewed in the hindsight!"

XXX

Table of Contents

20. *Human Society Is Not Different From Life In Wilderness*

Enter Protagonist

While still in standard four, studying at the town *Paathshaalaa*, I had little inkling about the nefarious innate nature of fellow human beings and playmates or classmates. By that time I could not imagine in my wildest dreams that anybody could steal another fellow's belongings, least of all a friend's, a classmate's.

When I was in standard four our father, though a draconian creature still, had not yet turned a wretch; he was still on the rolls of the High School there albeit in an *ad hoc* capacity, of which, we -- or even he himself – took little cognizance. Being a teacher, he took every care to ensure provision of required books, notebooks, geometrical instruments etc. for my studies, and I could never apprehend that in near future there might come even a time when I would be shorn of all those facilities and would even crave the notebooks or even a single paper for writing thereon.

My father had bought me an attractive as well as sturdy mathematical compass made of brass – of golden or brass colour. I was so possessive of that item, and used to flaunt it before my classmates and playmates time and again, little realising that such acts of valour or pomp seldom attracted appreciation of the fellow human beings, rather they resulted in engendering envy in the hearts of the latter, especially, those who were paupers or those belonging to lower strata of society.

I myself had been wallowing in the glory of my valuable compass thinking that none else had had such a valuable instrument except me, taking myself for a rich and special creature.

After a few days, nonetheless, I found that my compass was missing; it had been stolen from my bag by somebody. I was stunned and felt crest-fallen at this mishap. I could not imagine that someone of my fellow students might have stolen it: I didn't know yet the name of the game of theft or stealing. How could someone steal – acquire unrightfully the right to use – another person's articles, least of all the schooling gadget, the study material. I felt sad at my carelessness and sense of loss – first ever in my life – at this happening. When I brought this fact to the notice of my parents, as usual, my kind-hearted mother was sympathetic and assured me that she would arrange another compass for me, but the father was disparaging

as well as critical remarking that I was so callous and careless as ever, and also, he did not give me any assurance that he would buy me another compass.

I had to make do with a commonplace aluminium compass thereafter which had lesser propensity to be stolen by scoundrels. I learnt by deduction that commonplace possessions were the safest possessions; in the same vein I learnt in later life that the commonplace – medium sort of – lady is the safest lady for making one's wife. I now possessed a commonplace compass like all others in the melee had! And that commonplace character of the compass proved to be a guarantee that nobody would steal it anymore.

Nonetheless, I could never help missing my golden coloured compass. Somewhere in the deep of my heart I had a hunch that the fellow pretending to be my fast friend – that low caste fellow whose father was a barber of our family – might have made away with my valuable instrument. For, he had given me the impression that stealing valuable things from others was not such a big deal or a moral hazard at all: that was his value system! His family members also harboured such notions.

Whereas I was reeling under the grief of my lost compass, one day when I was sharing notes of study with my friend – the same wily fellow – I noticed that he was using the same compass, the bright brass or golden coloured one. I immediately felt that I had got my compass but that was not to be: that was no more mine one, that had been possessed and owned by the thief now. After theft, the ownership of articles gets transmuted to the thief from the real owner! I could do nothing! It felt like my fiancée had been snatched away surreptitiously or stolen by someone and I could do nothing, for now she was the usurper's property.

I could neither make a comment that the compass was mine one, nor could I claim it back from my sham friend: for he pretended to be my fast friend. Whither fast friend! However, I still can reminisce that friendly betrayal with a sense of loss and friendly betrayal.

Nevertheless, the crooked fellow feeling guilt conscience or the qualms of conscience himself started commenting that his elder uncle – who was the money manager of their household – had bought him the compass. Despite knowing fully well that he was lying and that his mere commenting on the acquisition of that compass went to prove without doubt that he had stolen the same from my bag. Guilt conscience never lets go of the guilty offender throughout his or her life.

I felt so sad and sorry about the composition of society and world and was face to face with the insurmountable wall of questions as to how to survive such onslaught on the possessions and property of honest individuals by the unscrupulous fellows. But to no avail. I have still today not found any answer to this intractable question of the creation and human world. The human society is not different from the life in the wilderness at all.

This childhood episode reminds me of the happenings having taken place during my son's schooling days. We purchased valuable pens, pencils etc. thinking that our son should not feel inferiority complex, but the senior students in his school used to steal all such things the next day from his bag, to the dismay of the innocent child and the misplaced and unreasonable rage of us parents. Not only this, the elder students did not let him take a seat in the school bus as well, and also, did beat him. Smelling something fishy, one day we took a plunge and raided the classroom in the absence of the students when they were in the Assembly and eventually recovered all the stolen stuff from the bags of the thieves. We took all the stuff to the Head Master and brought to his notice the gory act of stealing rampantly, also the fact of torturing of innocent little kid by hooligans in the bus. Contrary to our expectation, the Head Master objected to our action of having rummaged through the bags of students in latters' absence and having recovered most of the stolen articles. When we resented, he budged and called the guys who confessed to stealing and torturing the small guy. After getting scolding by the Head Master, they mended their ways and no such incident took place thereafter.

Nonetheless, my heart aches: not for my beloved child, but for all those innumerable kids who are subjected to such tortures and thefts of seemingly trifling articles, and their parents punish them only for no fault of theirs, instead of taking action against scoundrels and bullies. The Nature shall ever be like that: bullies shall torture the gentle and polite!

XXX

Table of Contents

21. Hospitality Left To The Child's Mercy

Enter Mother

Those — especially the grown-ups in the feudal set-ups -- who think that they can do without taking any pains at doing anything personally including hospitality towards their equally arrogant and conceited relatives must needs learn a lesson from this tale.

As mentioned heretofore umpteen number of times, my in-laws had a family fiefdom, a feudal setup: no freedom for womenfolk, little freedom for childish activities of youngsters, fake sense of self-aggrandisement despite in essence being hollow money-wise, even intellectually. My in-laws had all their relations without exception who could stake their claims to such conceited grandeur. Apparently they looked so outwardly, given their majestic mansions and their clouts in their respective areas. But that was before the '*Aazaadee*'! When they had a free run to exploit the majority paupers under their suzerainty! Not anymore!

They seldom visited us: may be their sense of superiority forbade them from visiting this family whom the former might be thinking inferior to their stature in society or hierarchy. Yet, some of them were still there who happened to visit this family – our in-laws – sparingly, whenever they might be feeling nostalgic about their foregone days of grandeur which had since slipped from their grip after '*Aazaadee*'. One such relative of ours – an old grand personage of his area, a wealthy and prosperous landlord or, so to say, a warlord – once happened to visit this village. Those were the days of monsoon and the climate was sultry as well as extremely humid. Very uncomfortable. For both young and old. At such an unwelcome moment the old man opted to visit our family.

My husband as usual was extraordinarily enthused to show his hospitality towards his relative – the husband of his father's elder sister. My husband would have been obliged to this old man given the former's incorrigible habit to borrow money from everybody whoever came his way including relatives, even close relatives. Nonetheless, my husband, as he did not believe in exerting himself personally even in the matters of hospitality to be offered to his adorable relatives, ordered me in the noon to prepare food or feast for the old man. As was my wont as well or the tendency to hate whatever or whoever was related to this feudal family of indolent and insolent creatures, I obliged by grunting and muttering all sorts of abuses towards both my husband and the *oldie*. Yet there was no option but to fall in line with my husband's commands.

As already indicated heretofore, our male residences were quite afar from the residences of females – at a stone's throw, although. I cooked the feast or food whatever one would like to call it to my best abilities. In the tortuous weather of July or August.

Now, who would fetch the plates full of food and dishes from house to the male residence? My husband expected every chore to be done by someone else except himself. He loved to be seen himself as sitting idle and using his tongue merely ordering and commanding others. Had the women been allowed, he would have expected me to take the plates to the male residence and serve. However, the convention and prohibitions of feudalism did not permit it and my husband was a staunch follower of all things feudal and related to fiefdoms. He, therefore, shifted that responsibility to my small bodied toddler who was hardly six or seven years old albeit school-going. The weather being inclement and the timings being unwelcome – of noon time – my son showed his reluctance to oblige, for he was either studying his school books or was busy playing something all alone or with someone of his playmates, I can't recollect. But he was dead against carrying all that load unto the *Khedaa*. His excuse as he uttered was that the items of the plate might come tumbling down if he stumbled or swaggered on the way. He might be right but the conceptions of grown-ups, especially, in the feudal set-ups do not take such truths in their stride. They think that whatever they think is the *shaastra-pramaan* (Gospel truth). This attitude also showed their lack of depth of knowledge about the world and the life *per se*. In that respect, the natural instinct of a child might be truer. And it did.

When there was delay in fetching the food, my husband came rushing huffing and puffing, fretting and fuming, to be precise, as though the auspicious time was about to pass for performing that holy task of eating the food. As usual, he made faces, warped his eyebrows and uttered some obscene abuses against me and my kid as usual. Ultimately he made away with the *Thaalee* towards the *gher*.

But the helpings had to be constantly supplied after that first serving. And those had been left by my husband to the mercy of my little kid still. Who was already loath to such errands of elders. That too, at such odd hours! The little kid actually had little regard for family affiliations, more so, for those concerning grown-ups. After much cajoling, I could bring my kid to the point of making him agree that he would take the *chapaatees* or dishes, putting them on the plate covered by another plate. Nonetheless, this rigorous duty involved repetition of this job multiple times – till the guest was done with his eating. The little kid obliged two times and successfully, though grunting and taking it as an avoidable hassle, rather, an imposition by elders of their own duties on the younger ones. Whereas my husband and his father were glad sitting beside the

influential guest at the *chaupaal,* my little kid was lugging around discharging an onerous and tough duty: for no good of himself, rather, of those two elders who were good for nothing. The guest was all the more useless going by the perspective of the little kid!

The third time after much cajoling and persuasion when he was carrying the plate with *chapaatees* to the *chaupaal* - which was on an elevated mud platform in fact, and for scaling that height almost half a dozen steps were required to be traversed – all made of mud and rugged stones and in a state of utter disrepair – he stumbled against a jagged stone of the step and the plate came crashing down – *chapaatees* falling one side, the plate the other. There was a loud bang as well, as the metal – brass – plate fell down and rolled over down the steps. But the duo elder males were too busy and complacent to conceive of such mishaps at the hands of an inexperienced and unwilling servant as my kid, and they indeed did not hear the sound – neither of the plate nor of the *chapaatees* falling down.

The little boy unaware of the implications and horrors of a fallen *chapaatee* and plate on the dust and trash of the soil, where cattle did urinate and defecate day and night, quickly gathered the plate and the *chapaatees* and, after clearing those of any dust particles, resumed his service of a bearer and supplied the *chapaatees* to the *oldie*. He gave no sign of any embarrassment or bewilderment at all on reaching there. He, however, waited in attendance at the guest to see the repercussions of the mishap – to see whether it did make any difference to the taste of the guest when it came to eating the fallen and retrieved *chapaatee* all smeared with the urinated trash.

And on having his first bite of the *chapaatee* the guest had a nauseating feeling; he said, the *chapaatee* was having dust and stones in it. My husband and his father could not make out anything of that. They could never ever in their dreams imagine that the *chapaatees* would have fallen down and more horribly retrieved from the night soil of the domestic cattle, and might have been served nonchalantly and without any qualms of conscience. Only the little kid knew the reality of the world at that moment. He was bemused at the folly of the grown-ups and was deriving a perverse pleasure at the revenge he had taken upon his father who, instead of serving the guest himself by ensuring that the eatables reached safely and securely, was depending on a quack, a kid, who did not have any idea about the difference between a human's food and a cattle's urine.

There is a saying in our village: *'chor se mor marvaanaa'* (to assign a thug the duty to guard the treasure). The feudal setup lacked that common sense and they lost face before the guest. The guest condescended by pretending that he had had his full and needed no more and gave up eating forthwith. The males duo also thought that nothing unusual had happened. They simply thought that there might have been some stone in the flour by oversight. They enquired of the kid cursorily if the plate had fallen down. As a child he had no option but to say emphatically that nothing of that sort had happened; when the elders themselves could not be so attentive as to listen to the banging sounds arising on the way from house to the *Gher* – the *Khedaa*.

My husband though did not make much fuss about it, he did not learn any lesson either out of this episode; that was his sort of stuff. He never learnt anything as he thought that whatever he did or thought was the only perfect thing.

I, however, concluded on learning of this incident from the mouth of my son later on that hospitality of guests should never be left to the mercy of children, nor of the attendants. They might play spoilsport if only unintentionally and innocently.

XXX

Table of Contents

22. The String Of Death

Enter Maamaajee *(Elder Maternal Uncle)*

I harbour a notion in my heart that children must be kept under tight control and strict discipline; then only some sense of sanity can be instilled in the family. All the babies or toddlers or children – of whatever age – feared me like anything. I was a devil incarnate for the children of not only our close family but others as well. Wherever I sighted children – either solo or in company – I definitely found a pretext to rebuke them ferociously and mercilessly. The result was that children did not dare face me or cross my way. Another trick to discipline the family drove was to engage them in some wearisome errands thereby disrupting their interesting games or plays.

On one such occasion, during the dusk – it was monsoon season and it had just stopped raining – I found that the children were merry-making all around creating ruckus. I immediately thought of a knavery and commanded them to follow me: to the agricultural fields, which we had aplenty. The pretext was to fetch fodder for the cattle – green crops for fodder. The field intended for visiting was somewhat distant. Two of the kids followed me – the son of my sister and the son of my younger brother – for I forbade the rest – mainly girls and small kids – from

following us. All the three of us made to the pathway towards that intended destination with sickles or scythes in our hands and waist clothes on our bodies. It was a humid and sweltering atmosphere at that hour of the day, afternoon, that is. I knew that the two children were not amused with this unwarranted distraction in their cheerful merry-making at the dusk. No child would like to be disturbed while engrossed in the games with playmates. But I relished such tyranny towards children; that was my wont.

In that wet atmosphere when there were puddles of water and mud all around and that too on our pathway, we were wading through the head-high overgrowth of crops – millet - and green vegetation all around. The sun was yet to set as though waiting for our chore to be completed first. We were hardly one or two fields afar from our destination when we were traversing a dense overgrowth and were constantly pushing aside the fallen crops – which had fallen under their weight in the wake of heavy rains -- from our path to make way for us to proceed.

Suddenly, it was exactly in front of us: a cobra rushing towards us on the same singularity of the pathway on which we three were, hardly able to push ourselves forward with no scope for evading the oncoming commuter, a seven foot long yellowish cobra with its hood raised high towards the sky. It was me in the front; following me was my nephew and at the fag-end was the only son of my sister.

No sooner had I raised an alarm with a bursting and shrieking shout sounding like a cry than the poor creature was upon us, sort of caught between a rock and a hard surface. The poor (?) creature as well had no time or choice to revert or go astray in that straitjacket situation of the pathway. Nor was there time enough to manoeuvre our steps or strategies. I was making all sorts of tantrums and tricks and noises to shoo away the venomous creature who was by this time ensnaring our legs and I was desperately trying to push my co-travellers onto the overgrowth impenetrable. Those few seconds – hardly 10 seconds or so – of interface with that string of death – *yamaraaja* himself – seemed like an aeon having elapsed. Those 10 seconds were not allowing themselves to be passed; as though the time had stopped, as though the space had collapsed, as though we were caught inside a blackhole, a singularity. We were crying and trying as though we were dying collectively; all the three of us!

However, that travel through the tunnel of blackhole passed somehow with all of us absolutely shaken and unaware of our physical state and fate, whether we were bitten by the venomous snake or were let unscathed by grace of Providence. The bewildered cobra itself had somehow released itself from this unexpected serpentine enmeshing with the legs of three innocuous human species. It had not thought it necessary to use its fangs to inject the fatal venomous juice into our permeable legs. It seemed as if it was equally embarrassed and non-plussed at this unexpected encounter of a reptilian species with the progeny of species of homo sapiens

The death's messenger had not used its weapon to finish us off, yet I was unsure about this fact. In such an stampede sort of situation I was sure and certain that the snake would have bitten someone of us. After its hiding in the overgrowth I examined the bodies of both the children and enquired of them repeatedly if they were feeling like having been bitten by the snake, whether they were feeling sleepy or drowsy – I was given to understand that a man bitten by a poisonous snake feels like sleeping, feels drowsy – whether there was any pain in any limb of their physical bodies etc.

The boys tried to find answers to my incoherent questions by examining their bodies which seemed unscathed outwardly at least, but who knows what's the fact, for none of us had been bitten by a snake before in our lives; we had no prior experience of snake-bite or how it felt like on being bitten by a seven feet long snake, or at the time of dying by snake-bite. For that 10 seconds' encounter, or nightmare, to be true, I did undertake a *post-facto* check-up of our human bodies for 10 minutes at least. How fragile the human body is! How ephemeral it is! Our pretty carnal corporeal self which we consider so immortal and invaluable! That we adore so much! It could vanish within no time! Every wild creature of the Nature, the wilderness, has that power! To finish it off – the human body!

To my bewilderment, whereas my nephew who was immediately behind me was aware that it was a snake that had created such a mayhem amongst us, the son of my sister who was taking the rear of the single file of us three did not know the cause of our crying and shouting and pushing around the overgrowth. He asked innocently, "What was that, I didn't see it?"

I revealed to him, "It was a dreaded snake, a cobra and it got entangled in our legs". He was not alarmed nonetheless, for he had not had a glance at the snake, rather, he felt bemused as if we were lying and amusing ourselves in the manner of concocting the serpentine story.

In the process, the sun god too felt it expedient to set swiftly now, because there was no point in its staying put in the sky at that height when we had dropped our plan to fetch the fodder from the field. We immediately set off on our return journey to our village, towards our home, the purpose of this hurry being to make it doubly sure that our assessment of our fragile bodies not having been bitten by the cobra despite close shave was really correct. In the village we had the advantage of other seasoned elders who had at least the remote knowledge of snake-bites in respect of their acquaintances, and also, their ultimate fate eventually, if not the experience of themselves having been bitten by snakes and cobras.

What the two lads were contemplating on return journey I cannot say – they must be deriving perverse pleasure from my having learnt a crude lesson in ferocity and dread: the cobra was still more ferocious and more dreadful than I ever pretended to be myself. Moreover, their curse that they might be conceiving against me on the spoiling of their childish games at that hour of dusk had fructified and they were back to their games, thus were happy again. But, throughout the way on return journey I kept on thanking God Almighty for salvaging my honour for, had something untoward happened to either of those two lads

– one was my brother's son and the other one was my youngest sister's only son – I would not be able to show my face to the world. My sister's son was the only son, she having lost one son already to child mortality or possibly to the parental callousness.

At village, the episode became the staple of everyday chat in every household and at every male and female gathering for next few weeks. The view based on conventional and mythological wisdom emerged that the snake would have been some ancestor of ours who might have come to visit our fields during this monsoon season insofar as despite having come face to face with us and despite having passed through our feet and legs it had not thought it proper to bite us. The recompense suggested with the help of village priest was the solemnisation of a *Kathaa* (a prayer) in the honour of the serpentine ancestor, as also, to propitiate the aggrieved ancestors who had had to visit our land for reminding us of our sins in the form of having forgotten them, or having become rude and arrogant towards children.

Now, the propitiatory ritual or function was held beside a well almost near the site of the snaky and shaky episode in an open field and people from nearby villages were called, too, to partake of the feast thrown to one and all, of course, after offering the share of snaky ancestors to them first of all. It was an interesting feat for the kids and children like us. After having done this ritual, I at least felt freed from the burden on my heart; I felt as though a heavy burden had been lifted from there.

I sometimes feel that these *karmakaandas* (rituals) if only they might have no scientific basis, are beneficial in the sense that they purge the mind of many a botheration that are engendered in the aftermath of such unforeseen and inconceivable incidents and mishaps. The whole gamut of rituals as envisaged in the *Shastras* and *Vedas* is not entirely meaningless or purposeless: it has its utility – at least for the mundane world, in this virtual, ephemeral world, if not in the real world, the world which is beyond our bounds and pale.

XXX

Table of Contents

23. Father's Domain And Dharmashaalaa

Enter Protagonist

My maternal grandfather's household and that of our father's one used to be intermingled in our childhood psyche: we could not differentiate between the two - their significance, so to say. In other words, we could not make out whether the maternal grandfather's house was our own house or the house of our father was our own house. In fact, there was no house owned by my father; he was homeless, shelterless! So far as we babies were concerned, we felt that *Naanee*'s house was our own house, for it was a sprawling large house and was surrounded by greenery and an atmosphere of pleasantness whereas the house at our father's village was a small room – rather, only half of that, since half of the room was shared with our *Taaeejee* – and there was no liberty to move outside of the house in the greenery or amidst the trees. It was like a jail in a sense: for us children and for womenfolk! That was the difference between a feudal living and a farmer's living style. Our father's side represented feudal one and our *Naanee's* side represented peasant's one.

My father did not own the responsibility of his wife and children on himself; he was carrying the family as though it were someone else's load. He therefore used to send the family and children to *Naanaa*'s home at the drop of a hat or a pin. Or whenever he was short of food grains and cereals. In those days, the concept of food as a balanced diet containing all the ingredients or nutrients required for the body was not known to us; food simply signified food grains or cereals – the *rotee*, the *chapaatees* --

as simple as that!

In this frequent parcelling off of the family from father's village to *Naanee*'s or *Naanaa*'s village or *vice versa*, one phenomenon was common that we observed so vividly: that on return journey, we invariably used to be made to stay in a *dharmashaalaa* at the nearby town which was beside a sweet shop owned by an acquaintance of our father's. In this process, sometimes the wait used to be quite long, and I wondered why our father had to resort to this *dharmashaalaa,* a tavern, as a sojourn during our journey home, and why he didn't fetch a bullock-cart or a tonga straightaway on our arrival from our *Nanihaal.* But father's financial status and social demeanour was like that only – perfectly *lack-a-daisical*! He didn't own a bullock-cart either, nor did his entire family own one; still paradoxically, they claimed themselves to be great, meaning thereby a wealthy pedigree. I wondered at these contradictions in apparent reality and the hollow talks of the family elders, particularly, of our father. Other commuters who alighted from the bus along with us used to depart straightaway, whereas here were we – us children and our helpless mother who was young and pretty by that time – who were made to wait there in the heat and dust of this *dharmashaalaa* every time whenever we happened to come back from *Nanihaal*. Actually, unto this *dharmashaalaa* only did our *maamaajee* use to accompany us and used to leave us at the *Dharmashaalaa* and would go back by return vehicle.

This sort of compulsive stay every time at *dharmashaalaa* of the town betrayed to me the inferiority of resourcefulness and lack of any worth on the side of my father. I started treating him as an unworthy father to a sensitive son, an unsuitable husband to a worthy, wealthy and virtuous lady. He was not harnessing his household sensibly and was just somehow pushing around dementedly and in a foolhardy manner. In my considered view, such unworthy lads should not be wed with the worthy ladies hailing from prosperous families.

XXX

Table of Contents

21. The Vanquished Aspect Of Humanity

Enter Protagonist

Though not situated in the orchard meant for our ancestors, *kuldevas* and *kuldevees*, yet another prominent deity for the family was *Chaamarh* or *Chaamadh*, to pronounce correctly. His memorial was located somewhat nearer to the hamlet but on the opposite side of the garden. The memorial consisted of an almost square platform, half a metre in height from the ground and supported with a few steps to climb onto it. In the middle of it, there was a heap of ash, smouldering cinders, some semi-burnt flowers and all sorts of queer items, offering an eerie spectacle to the awestruck eyes. Mostly ladies used to offer obeisance there, but male members too were seen paying tributes there on the platform of the *Chaamadh devataa*. The offering to *Chaamadh* used to be the fire, smouldering cinders, embers etc. I could not fathom the implications of adoration for this fire-eating god by my village-folk. The present day *Chamaars* logically seem to be the descendants of *Chaamarh,* and maybe because he was vanquished in the battle, their descendants are categorised as lower caste till date by the victors. These so-called lower castes are actually the vanquished aspect of humanity, vanquished and tortured in revenge by the victors in perpetuity.

As per scriptures, particularly, the *Durgaa Saptashatee, Chaamarh* was the ferocious daemon warlord in the army of *Mahishaasur* who fought against Mother goddess *Durgaa* alongside *Mahishaasur*. He was eventually vanquished and, in turn, killed by the lion of mother goddess by beheading him by the stroke of his paw. Why must my ancestors adore this daemon nonetheless, has ever remained a conundrum for me. However, presently in hindsight, I can well capture its significance in that my clan was a clan of martial folks and martial clans were all christened as daemons, *raakshasas*, particularly, if vanquished by the victorious side. This brave soldier would have been some unforgettable ancestor of ours or of our village in whose memory – so as to immortalise his valour and to inspire the generations to come – the worship by fire for this queer deity, continued. Of late, with the onslaught of dry reason on the culture, I find, that the platform and the deity, and also, the worship thereof, all have vanished, even as, the greedy peasant in whose farmland this spot fell has merged every bit of this mythological memorial in his field razing everything to ground.

The similar has long been the fate of the garden of *devataas* and *kuldevataas*. The wretched land-starved progenies of our prodigious ancestors have long since felled the entire orchard, sold off its lumber and thrown away all the memorials which we venerated so much without an iota of doubt in our hearts. It's now an agricultural field yielding a few quintals of cereal every year to the recorded owner of the land. As an orchard, it was supposed to be a common property of the entire family clan back then! In those munificent days!

Nonetheless, it now belongs to only one selfish family.

XXX

Table of Contents

25. Callous Conventions

Enter Naaib Saaheb

I was posted at *Sikandraabaad* those days as *Naaib Tehsildaar*. The town was not far from the village where my niece *Phool* was married. I am talking of 1960s and the social, political and economic milieu those days was entirely different from what it looks like today: there were no mobile phones – not even landline phones, to be true; there were no banks like those available these days; there were no cars around in our area, or even in the countryside generally; there were no means of conveyance and communication as are available these days *et al*. The life used to be simple, posing no complications for the living beings!

The Nature and life themselves were benign towards the living beings, yet the social and political milieu was tortuous to the worst possible extent. The superstitions, traditions or conventions – whatever you call them or name them – were ever on the neck and heart of the citizens. Traditions which lacked humaneness, which verged on the cruelty even perceptible to the naked eye, which apparently seemed to be lacking civility; still they claimed their civilization and society to be having very high standards! Woeful condition no doubt!

My niece had been wedded in that village almost ten years back, and I having been posted at *Sikandraabaad* felt it incumbent upon me to pay a visit to her village: that was the convention, no let-up therein could be brooked! Social norms were imposed with inviolable accuracy and strictness!

After dilly-dallying for quite a long time after having been posted there, I ultimately made up my mind to finish off this chore too – of course, after ensuring that I had acquired enough silver coins in my pockets for giving presents to every which one present there. That was the convention! Callous convention indeed! Everybody from young to adult to old was to be gifted some cash invariably; and every time whenever one visited the village of one's relatives!

As was the penchant and norm prevalent those days amongst the feudal set-ups, my niece was married in a feudal family which was quite large, even by the standards of those days. And consequently, I had to arrange a hefty sum for 'gifting' first of all. The visit was at all a pleasant visit to a relative, rather, it smacked of a sentence to be suffered at the hands of vulgar society. Social set-up was indeed very problematic and

tyrannical in those days!

And at the same time contrastingly, the economic and financial scenario of both the high and low castes or creeds was pathetic; money was a rare commodity those days. Most of the human bodies were seen half naked those days, not only moving around, but also, visiting other villages in the same semi-naked pose or attire. In the name of money, the countryside had only cereals and grains to barter – no cash unlike it is in vogue these days. No question of digital money or digital payments! There were no ATMs or PayTMs, too!

After lot of thinking and rethinking, I made a visit: and that too only for a day, a single day. The relatives coming from the side of girl's parents were not supposed to eat or drink anything at their daughter's in-law's house. What a queer and abominable convention! What a bizarre relationship! The hidden agenda would have been to dissuade the relatives from the village of the daughter-in-law from visiting her and know her travails in the process. What an uncivilized society!

Since I was a *Tehsildaar*, even as, a *Naaib* one, and *Tehsildaar* was supposed to be a big gun in the countryside by those times – a hangover from the times of *British Raaj*, I was treated with extreme awe and respect at the village of *Phool*'s in-laws. Everybody was looking at me as if I were some superman! Nevertheless, I was worried about my pocket only that was soon to get depleted. I noticed that there was no end to the worthies who were eligible for getting *Bhaint* -- gifts -- from my hands at that household.

Let me clarify here, too, that some of those at the village also thought and were convinced that I was not a *Tehsildaar*, but an *Ameen* or a *Patwaaree* only. Nonetheless, in a countryside, it mattered little whether one was an *Ameen* or a *Patwaaree* or a *Tehsildaar*, one is proclaimed but as the senior-most functionary. Those antagonists took one as junior-most, and those favourably disposed took one as senior-most, irrespective of what the truth might be. Nevertheless, everybody claimed to be in the know of the truth! But they loved to live with their fabricated realities!

Somehow my visit was accomplished and a blemish of my not having visited the in-laws of my niece could be obliterated. At least for the present birth! There was no question of visiting that village again in my lifetime; there was no wherewithal available with me to repeat the same expensive visit and to revisit the same inhumane and superstitious social milieu.

XXX

Table of Contents

26. Neel Kothee *In The Wilderness*

Enter Protagonist

In my narration, I have been focussing on human beings only, leaving aside the natural phenomena by and large, as I see. Like the body of living beings – be these human beings or be these domestic cattle or be these wild beasts – all keep on changing shape, countenance and look continually yet they remain unobserved, without coming into notice of anybody: such is the slow motion of natural processes! Of the Creation! Result is apparent, yet the process is not visible at all. Conscious creatures observe the change taking place unceasingly in every phenomena of the Nature, yet they can't discern the process taking place with their open eyes or senses. The seasons keep on changing without exception and keep on repeating themselves at annual frequency, too; weather keeps on changing every day, nay every moment; vegetation keeps on changing every season and every day almost. Nothing is unchangeable around us: everything is cropping up and withering away with a definite regularity as well as certainty.

Likewise, I observe that the landscape I am referring to is totally transformed during this huge gap of my lifetime: from childhood to this old age, from my school days to this retirement's leisure time, from those days of so many aims to attain yet to these days of ennui and boredom without anything to attain or gain. Those days, the distance between our small village to the town was mostly barren; it's not so these days: these days, not even an inch of soil is seen barren; people grow crops on every inch of land which was seen lying vacant and uncared for those days. Starting with a brook of water that flowed in the vicinity of our village and was the pride of people of our hamlet and of envy for the people of neighbouring hamlets, we used to pass by an orchard abounding in fruit trees mostly of guava, mango, *Jaamun*, lemon etc.

In fact, the garden seemed to be quite large by the eyes of us children, giving us the feeling of a wilderness in the vicinity of our village, and also, it engendered a sense of fear and scare in our hearts while passing by it. It was actually on both the sides of the dusty path leading to the town that we traversed and was a source of inexplicable pleasure for us children. We don't recollect whether ever we had the chance to eat any fruit from the trees of these orchards, nevertheless, mere idea of an orchard being there on our way to the school filled us with the fancy that one day we could get to have and eat plentiful of guavas, *Jaamuns* and mangoes from those trees. However, it was never to happen; the human beings who claim to be the owners – or occupants, to be true – of these God-given bounties were not so kind or considerate as to offer fruits to the passers-by, especially, the innocent and aspirant kids who didn't own any such bounties and used to fancy in their childish ways such magnanimity on the part of grown-ups. Grown up people, nonetheless, have always proved to be very mean as all the children of all the lands could vouchsafe.

Beyond the orchard, then there was a pond – a water reservoir – a *Pokhar*, which was a resource of water for the village cattle and other wild creatures, and also, a resource of black and sticky clay for the village folks for constructing as well as repairing their habitats or dwelling units that were mainly thatched *kutcha* huts. The *Pokhar* was a resort for merry-making for the children as well; we could take a cold bath in that pond while returning from the school in the hot summer noons, however, unbeknown to our parents. The water was extremely dirty and slimy, but dirtiness or being unhygienic were none of the factors of our concerns those days; in that sense, the entire scenario looked dirty only all around to us children. Well, in that dirty swamp of the pond there were the lotus flowers blooming in the season and we children plucked their roots – *kamal naal* -- even as, we were given the impression, by whom I don't know, that the roots of lotus – *kamal naal* -- were very beneficial for health. Nevertheless, in this *lotusy* adventure there were intertwined the risks of serpentine ensnares, too. The water snakes were also sighted by us there oftentimes. But some of us children warded off our fear by proclaiming that the water snakes were not poisonous or dangerous. Poisonous or not poisonous, mere sight of those stringy creatures resembling death gave a chill and dread in the spine!

In our childish conviction, we assumed that our watery adventures in the insanitary as well as unhealthy pond would not be detected by the members – elders – of our families, but invariably every time they could detect our misadventure at first sight, on the entry to our homes itself. And we were baffled to think as to how those grown-ups came to know of the secrets of kids so easily: we wondered if they were wizards or accomplished sages having attained some *siddhees* of the kind.

Beyond the swampy pond, there was a small bridge – a *Puliyaa* – and then a bridge which was in bad state of repair, its side boundaries having been dismantled, its bricks having been stolen by poor if only greedy village folk. This relatively bigger bridge was supposed to be on the brook flowing underneath it, but in our lifetime – or even during our school days - we never saw that brook having a drop of water flowing therein. It used to be a dry ditch, and the bullock-carts – that was the only mode of conveyance in those olden days – or the horse-carts that passed thereby, used to take the route not over the bridge but bypassing it through the non-existent brook , even as, it was as level and plain as the remainder of the dusty path. Of course, all around that point there were wild bushes, wild vegetation beside a few agricultural fields, as well.

The fields in the vicinity of this bridge belonged to my friend's father. I used to go to school with this kind and affable friend daily. And while returning from the school, mostly at noon or in the afternoon, we found the sisters of this friend sitting at the bridge; they were there in connection with some agricultural or household chores. They were quite affable and kind to us both and we got very happy and felt a sense of safety whenever we found them present there. Their presence there filled us both with a sense of security in that seeming wilderness all around. The wilderness seemed dangerous from the standpoint of us kids, though for the adults there was no such thing as dangerous about this innocuous spot. Incidentally, my friend and his sisters had lost their mother sometime back and thus sisters had assumed the role of their brother's mother as well as caretaker, too.

From this bridge, the distance of our town was just equal to the distance of our village from there. On reaching the bridge we small kids felt pleased and heaved a sigh of relief thinking that there onwards our destination was only half the distance.

Passing through the crops and wilderness in an unsystematic pattern, we could see from some distance some brick-works, concrete constructions somehow in ramshackle state. People used to tell us, as did my father as well, that the constructions were the *Neel Kothees*. *Neel Kothee*, later on when we grew up, was one of those notorious contrivances of the colonisers that ultimately became the tool of tyranny on and exploitation of gullible peasants and which cause *Mahaatmaa Gaandhee* took up in *Bihaar* which finally resulted in whetting the fire of national movement in the country, and culminated in the exodus of *Britishers*. Such an historical building! And it was lying deserted! Proclaiming the travails of time! For both living and non-living creatures!

On one such absurd day, some of us kids gathered courage and visited the site, the *Neel Kothee*.

However, it was very large as against our perception created when seeing from afar. It looked dreadful as well even at the time we visited it. However, we wondered why nobody had dismantled the same whereas the colonisers had abandoned the place and the country almost over a decade back. The peasants having their fields in the vicinity did not touch this building for decades together, or it might be said that they could not muster courage to do so. Ultimately, they took away the bricks, used them and converted the *Neel Kothee* into arable agricultural fields. Today, there is no trace of any *Neel Kothee* at that spot. Not only every phenomenon of Nature is undergoing change unceasingly, but also, the constructs of human beings are ephemeral and have been undergoing definite transformation which becomes perceptible with open eyes after lapse of some time.

Beyond the *Neel Kothee* and almost in the vicinity of the town somewhat off the official route there were fields of vegetable and spice growers. The trodden path -- as it was somewhat short -- passed through these fields, to the chagrin of the field-owners. These fields spread around 10 to 12 acres of land were a sight worth seeing: all greenery, in all the seasons, aroma of raw spices of variegated sorts. Although the fields were kept under watch by the keepers so as to avert the eventuality of spices getting stolen or eaten by the passers-by, little kids sometimes made it away with a pinch of aniseed or coriander which had special attraction both as regards aroma and as regards taste even when eaten raw.

In the rural area, particularly, villages throughout the length and breadth of the country, I have nowhere seen farmers growing vegetables and spices; and have always wondered, why this paradox. Farmers have large tracts of land, they have wherewithal, they must needs consume the vegetables to avert cancerous growth of cells in the carnal body, still nowhere throughout the country any farmer normally grows vegetables; they simply grow cereals, pulses and some cash crops. Under some unwritten constitution as though! Near our town when we saw these vegetable fields replete with vegetables of all sorts, so seductive to our eyes and soul, we used to cherish this small patch of journey to our school. The growers of these vegetables were not in fact the farmers, they were townsfolk and they had vegetable and spice growing only as their family business *a la Varn Vyavasthaa* – the division of professions – which transformed into castes eventually. Under the unwritten constitution, if now, any other farmer except these vegetable growers raised such crops as these, that would be against the ethics of society, the *Varna Vyavasthaa!*

Spices are in fact herbs: in *Sanskritic* volumes and olden books they are called as herbs and connote a very welcome implication, something curing the diseases and keeping the body fit and healthy. That is why herbs formed part of the diet itself. In due course, with the advent of aggressors when they arrived here, they could not fathom the real import of the herbs and thought those to be something adding to the taste of the food items cooked. Tasty, of course, they make the cooked items, but that was not the purpose of adding herbs to the vegetables or food. Later on, these herbs got called spices and the entire import of the healthy herbs was lost in due course. That shows how a healthy tradition assumes the proportions of an unhealthy habit. Taken in modicum quantities and in raw or natural form, the spices, that is, herbs serve the purpose of keeping the machine called body in good repair and in fine fettle, but taken as processed items and with admixture of several unnatural ingredients, the spices become injurious to health of society as well as human beings.

XXX

Table of Contents

27. Deprivations All The More

Enter Protagonist

However benevolent the Creator of this universe might be, and however magnanimous He might be in His bounties showered in the shape of natural gifts given gratuitously to the living beings begotten on this planet, Earth, the set-up or social system that has been created by the human beings for co-existence of fellow humans and other creatures, supposedly inferior to the former, is quite iniquitous as well as downright partisan. Whether the inequities that have evolved on the surface of the planet are the deliberate contrivances of the wily human beings or are these the outcome of the inherent inequalities of various individuals as regards their skills and stamina, or, so to say, the convictions they harbour concerning co-existence of fellow beings on this planet, is a matter of much debate. Those who are better off offer the former logic, whereas those not so lucky choose to offer the latter one, however, to salvage their prestige in the eyes of fellow inhabitants of the planet.

It makes little difference if one is the best entity as regards brain power, and a proven prodigy as regards academic achievements or excellence; one might find oneself deprived of all those amenities and provisions that others with lesser brain power might get or avail.

Along with me did accompany one of my cousins to the school at town. His father was employed in Govt service, with Railways, though. His father had probably opted to keep his family at village in the company of his parents. The hidden conundrum behind this decision was that the lady had been at loggerheads with his husband *ab initio*, that is, since their marriage, and in turn, this was due to a trifling issue that could pretty well be ignored. The gentle and docile wife had, however, demanded to purchase glass bangles for her bare hands, and may be unintentionally, the husband being from a male chauvinistic feudal background as if to impress his wife in a negative manner, commented evasively, "Oh, what's the use of bangles? This is all wastage!"

This mirthful prank on the part of her newlywed companion called husband was too much for the pious lady. The bangles are supposed to be the guarantee for longevity of the husband. The wife got inexorably estranged with her husband forever thence. She never bore the bangles thereafter; her wrists remained bare lifelong. The grapevine has it that she bore the bangles only when, after many decades, his son got employed as a teacher in a school and bought his mother the much maligned bangles.

But the charm of the bangles that was supposed to have been derived at the young age had already diminished inexorably. Wearing bangles at that advanced age was of little use and served no purpose, I think. Such was the determination and self-esteem of an Indian lady!

Anyway, those days, or at least that year, his or her son used to accompany me to the town school. I used to visit his part of the household – the *Baakhar* – for collecting him for the school. And it was as if a norm that he was never found ready; I had to wait on him for some time invariably. Maybe I was going before time, too long in advance for school!

During this waiting period I used to notice that the grandmother of my friend, my cousin, was seen cooking dry fruits in the milk for him. Seeing those costly items that were beyond even my imagination, or whose names I even did not know, what to speak of aspiring to eat, I used to feel how wretched a life I was leading, also, conversely, how lucky my cousin was. Concomitantly, this also raised a question in my heart: why so much inequality in the fate-lines of children? This pathetic situation definitely impacted my psyche; I developed an inferiority complex. Not only an inferiority complex, but also, an ill-will towards my father thinking that he could afford nothing

of such luxuries and dry fruits. For, at my virtual hutment, I felt that even arranging two meals somehow was a big issue for my father, and he was never comfortable in this behalf throughout his long life. On the contrary, there was an atmosphere created by my father which was tortuous for us without exception. Even the two morsels of food we could not eat peacefully if the father was around in the house. He was like a wild beast who were as though ever in rage!

And my cousin, despite being blessed by Nature with a lesser brain than I was with, did savour variety of such items almost daily. Not only this, even during fairs being held at the town whenever we ran into our father, the latter would entertain my cousin to the neglect of mine. That filled me with rancour even towards my friend. My father did this to establish himself as an altruistic person, and to impress his cousins, in turn, but to no avail; he was marring my zeal and zest for life and gaining nothing in return from those already well off, his relatives whose ward my class or school fellow was.

Such incidents verging palpably on the accentuated feeling of deprivation necessarily lead to the tendency of greed in the issues of such parents who cannot afford even the basic necessaries of life. And it reflected in variegated instances of our childish behaviour. For instance, and that is merely for citing one out of so many others though sounding trifling, the other day there came a marriage party in our village as those did normally every year, for there was no dearth of young girls attaining puberty as well as marriageable age every year. There was no helping the progress of Time and that of the attainment of puberty of girls and boys as a consequence. Irrespective of whoever's marriage party it was we the teenagers thought it as our duty – and a right -- to help the elders in serving the marriage party during the feasts; and the feasts those days continued for several days, minimum being three days. We were not called upon to offer that gratuitous service, rather, we had ourselves taken upon ourselves the onerous task of helping every which family in whose family a girl was getting married. We would be serving water in the clay glasses; we would be serving *Raayataa* (spicy butter milk) in the *Sakoraas* (wide-mouthed clay bowls); and we would be serving any other item as per the dictates and wisdom of the elders present on the scene. In our childish notion we could never think that it was none of our business to be there beside the marriage party or the marriage functions. In fact the spur for that enthusiasm emanated from the certainty that our helping actions would entitle us to partake of the sumptuous feasts that were being offered to the marriage party. The titillation of the many types of sweats wrapped in silver foils would be so unrestrainable! This is also a fact that normally and in majority of the cases nobody even objected to our child-like demeanours; they allowed us to partake of the feasts unconcerned who at all we were.

Nonetheless, on one such occasion, when the marriage party of the daughter of *Bhaiyaajee,* the elder cousin of my father and a friend, arrived in our village, we children took zealous part in all sorts of chores associated therewith. And obviously, we thought we were entitled to the feasts! Out of various feasts, however, during one feast on one afternoon, when after the marriage party proper had finished taking their food, and the stripes had been cleaned, when the members of the village community – the serving folks -- started taking places on the stripes, we children also took our places without at all realizing that we had no right to such feasts unless invited specifically by the hosts. Being children, we thought that every child was equally entitled to all the feasts irrespective of whose family it belonged to or whoever was hosting them. My father was chit-chatting with *Bhaiyaajee* at that moment, possibly congratulating him on successful solemnization of the wedding of his youngest daughter, implying thereby that he had been relieved of the worry of arranging marriage of his youngest daughter at last. The responsibility of arranging marriage for daughters was such a tedious task, especially, in the wake of despicable evil of dowry! When my father saw me sitting there on the stripes and readying myself unassumingly for partaking of the sumptuous feast, immediately he jumped into action and vehemently forbade me from doing so; he was rather sort of shocked to see that without any invitation from the hosts a member of his family was availing the facility of having feast. I was rather shocked, too, to see that reaction of my father; I was rather thinking that my father would also partake of the feast, for I thought that he was there for that purpose only. I did not however budge from the spot, for other companions of mine did not; their guardians were not there albeit. When I did not budge, *Bhaiyaajee* himself ventured to suggest that there was no harm children taking feast uninvited; albeit his facial expressions suggested quite the contrary. Then I realized that what we children were doing was unauthorized and that no host appreciated our nuisance and actions. But who had ever educated us on such finer points; for us children whole earth was our family:

'Vasudhaiva Kutumbakam!'

One salutary effect of that day's objection by my father was, nonetheless, that thereafter I stopped going to help the hosts in the marriage parties and also from partaking of feasts uninvited. So far so good!

XXX

Table of Contents

28. Baakhar *(Bifurcated)*

Enter Badee Ammaa *(elder Grandma)*

Let me narrate first of all the milieu in which our lives were being lived – the lives of womenfolk, in the family fiefdom of *Badwaalaas*. It was well before I had chosen to get my residence, that is, *pucca* house constructed in the same *Baakhar* with the gate towards the rear – the wilderness: away from the tumult and bustle of the whole habitat, where supposedly civilized *homo sapiens* did dwell. In the overly populated female residences of this feudal family there were in fact three sets of habitats: in one set or *Baakhar* did live the family and progenies of the eldest grand old man, one of the four brothers of the broad family tree; in another such set or *Baakhar*, there lived the family and progenies of the youngest of the four proverbial brothers; in third set did live – though not jointly – the families and progenies of the two brothers in between. The *Baakhars* being sprawling settlements notwithstanding, the pressure of increasing number of issues, the kids, with every passing 'nine months' did get increasingly unbearable on all the four families. There was no check on the procreation of issues – number of them – by an individual couple; the more the better seemed to be the motto, the norm, or the accepted philosophy of the times, rather. Maybe in the backdrop of possibility of annihilation of entire populace in the wars and battles that could rage any time unbidden!

The power of procreation bestowed by the Creator on conscious beings seems to have been exercised in the manners unbridled and to the extents unlimited: one can beget as many issues as one likes. Unmindful of its consequences! On the individual itself – the begotten, on oneself – the begetter, and also, on the society – the collective humanity - as a whole! Nonetheless, the Nature has set checks and balances in its scheme: it has one factor – the land or soil, so to say -- which is invariably inelastic. Why only land as well as soil, which is inelastic, each factor of Creation is inelastic, in pre-fixed quantities, measures; it can't be produced afresh, additionally!

With the ever multiplying population the living space gets constricted per individual in inverse proportion; also, the resources – the second factor – get scarcer. Why only land for living beings, the land for the dead of the *Muslims* and *Christians* does also get constricted with every passing of the day, and with every passing away of the living human beings. The once cozy and habitable dwellings of all the four brothers – the *oldies* - in the course of time reached ultimately that stage: when the tantrums as well as idiosyncrasies of various members of families living in the same small – since turned claustrophobic – space became unbecoming and unbearable for the other sober candidates of the same grove.

The episode of the foulest squabble between the wife of my husband's nephew and the temperamental '*Mukhiyaa*' narrated heretofore came as a last nail in the coffin of this long drawn concept of living together – as a joint family. Being the eldest living grandee of the *Baakhar* inhabited by our set of families, the psychological strain on me was all the more, the greatest, rather. The attainment of '*Aazaadee*' for the newly born nation had put additional burden on the feudal family: that of adjusting to the new norms of social as well as political set-up. The '*Aazaadee*' had in one fell swoop rendered the family shorn of all the created grandeur and authority that seemed so enduring and eternal in the pre-*Aazaadee* period. The subjects or the menial folks though did still show reverence as usual towards the members of the family, yet there was a palpable realization on the part of everyone grown up that the things didn't imply the same adoration, and that there was no solid backing now behind that behaviour of obeisance on the part of lower strata of the same society. That paradigm shift was no doubt very taxing, not only for the masters, but also, for the servants, the serfs, so to say figuratively. Now, to adjust to the new reality, the masters had started contributing their mite to the physical labour in household and agricultural chores alongside their employees – servants, *kameraas*, so to say in local parlance.

It was in this milieu that when my only son decided to construct for me a *pucca* portion of habitat within the same *kutcha* yet sprawling *Baakhar*, I counselled him to go for a secluded portion, away and further from all the bustle of the joint living. I wanted seclusion as well as mental peace; there was even no privacy in the *Baakhar* set-up. The young couples had to contend with faked or assumed 'privacy' while indulging in carnal chores, or for making love with their partners. Even at night! And that situation was suffocating for both elders and the youngsters, particularly, when the number of married couples was on the rise by the day, and already the married couples were too many in the *Baakhars*. There being no freedom or say in the affairs of household for the female folks, either for venturing out into the vegetation or for doing manual labour in the agricultural fields, majority of them perished in these suffocating environs: health-wise as well as psychologically. One can just imagine their condition by the mere fact that I, being the eldest lady in the family, too, felt suffocation despite enjoying ample amount of freedom of movement and say in all the family matters.

In the portion of the proverbial brother to our lot, there were two further divisions in the family tree: one half for my son, and in the other half, the two sons of my brother-in-law's. The portion was constructed in the shape of U. On the side of two tiny arms of U each, there lived the family of the elder son of my brother-in-law, and I all alone – my son being employed in Railways at far off place in *Raajasthaan*. The bottom portion of U - which was longer by those standards - was shared by all the three families including that of the younger son of my brother-in-law, that is, the parents of our protagonist – with the latter ensconced in between us two. My demeanour towards the latter was soft and benevolent, incidentally.

My husband had,

incidentally, long perished succumbing to a sudden cardiac arrest – that we named 'don't know what happened!' My son was away at that time! I used to feel all alone thereafter! The depression of living alone despite being in the midst of so many people was telling upon my psyche. I craved peace; I wanted no interference in my activities from any side.

My son and daughter-in-law used to visit me once in a year – during summer vacations of their kids – to settle the accounts concerning agriculture with the share-croppers. It was only for that short time that I felt that life was worth living at all, or full of liveliness. Blood relationships infuse so much miraculous energy in the nerves of a conscious being! On one such visit, my son started constructing a *pucca* house for me.

When the ground was being broken and the inmates came to know of the fact that the house to be constructed was to be a *pucca* one – of bricks and mortar – they sort of felt shocked; for all the constructions around the village were *kutcha* if only sturdy and robust. This step on the part of my son was a revolutionary step and attracted its share of criticism and libel as any revolutionary and unconventional step does and did. Nonetheless, we persisted in our pursuit. When the plinth was being

done, it was time to decide the gates and doors; and when family elders saw that the frame of the main gate of the house was being fixed towards the rear – where no soul resided – they again expressed awe and shock, and in graver manners. They even raised the bogey of advisably avoidable solitude and isolation for the old lady, that is, me. Of course, I had come of age and was susceptible to any unforeseen mishaps any time. Yet, who cares for the unseen and unknown! Everybody contemplates that one would be exceptional to such untoward and uncertain mishaps; and that such things are destined for souls other than themselves, to the exclusion of themselves, so to say!

One prominent reason for our insistence on keeping our face as well as door away from the family hub was the almost daily tantrums of the younger son of my brother-in-law who kept on beating his gentle and sober wife on the slightest excuse – mostly for extorting money from her, as if she were earning money, not he himself! Another reason was the contemptuous attitude of the wife of the elder son of my brother-in-law who had as a climactic episode had a squabble with the *'Mukhiyaa'*. I wanted to be spared of such unseemly spectacles; I could not take them anymore.

For laying the groundwork, for retrieving our portion in the habitat, half the middle hall – or the long room – had to be dismantled down in the middle, thereby exposing the side towards new construction open for some days. Also, there was no wall or support on that side. It was thought – and foolishly, of course – that with the raising of *pucca* wall on our side, the gaping space would be filled, and the middle room would be safe still. How foolish the adults could be in their suppositions and actions can be gauged from this action of ours!

Our portion got constructed and the impressive *Baakhar* started giving an eerie look presently with only three-fourths of the portion remaining as a joint unit in our *Baakhar*. Soon thereafter, for the family of elder son of my brother-in-law had already had a tussle with the family of *Mukhiyaa*, the family of *Mukhiyaa*, too, raised a wall towards their side, thus sequestering the half portion of the original *Baakhar*. The portion of my brother-in-law now became a *kutcha* claustrophobic thatched portion: one-fourth of the erstwhile sprawling and buzzing *Baakhar*. Inhabited by the families of our protagonist and that of his elder uncle. This was in 1966 – summer vacations.

XXX

Table of Contents

29. Father Ousted From The Town School
Enter Protagonist

When elder grandee's house – the secluded house - was being constructed, I used to witness this spectacular feat with awe and wonder: how the groundwork was being done, how the ditches almost the height of a grown up human being were dug out, how the broken glass pieces and other hazardous items of the neighbourhood that were finding no suitable place to dispose them of, were buried in the innards of the ground, the plinth etc. A new – new style – habitat was being constructed and it was a matter of extreme intrigue and puzzle for kids like me. We used to sit on the not-yet-raised very high walls of the brickwork and used to watch the masons convert the 'space' into the 'construct'; it gave us mental succour as though! At times, as was the wont of elders in that feudal set-up, some elders drove us away barking us off without provocation, by wondering as to what we were doing there, at which, we felt like asking him or her what he or she was doing there, in turn. But we were not endowed with physical strength yet, enough to proffer this riposte to the mindless adult species of the *homo sapiens,* particularly, of that vulgar, martial and feudal set-up.

My mother being the sister of elder grandee's – *Badee Ammaa's* – daughter-in-law was very fond of her and, it seems, the latter was as well fond of the former. When the *Daadee* could not be approached from the side of *baakhar* as easily as she did earlier on, my mother used to send me to her – to the rear – for enquiring about her well-being, or on the like errands. The *Ammaa* was a bit strict demeanoured old grandee and I dreaded her, albeit she never said any harsh words to me. For that matter, not only the *Ammaa,* but also, all the members of hers – her son and daughter-in-law - were strict natured when it came to us children; and none of whom we children did like. They were not likeable creatures, so to say. Whenever I used to muster courage to reach her portion on the rear of our habitat, *Badee Ammaa* invariably called me with the epithet '*Eh*, the son of so and so!.....'' inserting my father's name therein derisively.

Came the summer vacations after grade four; and as usual we headed towards our *Naanee's* village by the first available transport – that was a given. Our impudent as well as indolent father made no mistake in shifting his family burden at the earliest opportunity towards his in-laws as if he was avenging his marriage with their daughter. Too, he was heard grunting about it explicitly and not infrequently that he had been married prematurely and against his will, thereby devastating his career. And in the hindsight, it now looks genuine too,

for he could not do anything in his life or career despite having squandered everything he had inherited from the wealthy and prestigious ancestors, and also, that got in dowry: gold, silver, money, utensils, land, everything! And ultimately the village itself! He could not pass B. Ed. even, and, on the contrary, kept on harping on his degree of B.A. which proved to be of no avail ultimately, and he died an unemployed pauper, like any illiterate and rustic person would have! What use such sham education?

We went to *Nanihaal* and got absorbed in the relish of serenity and amenities obtaining thereat. I was already established as a brilliant student by then, and people feigned to regard me as such. I was relishing that new found glory – childish one, of course, no doubt!

I had little inkling at that time while absorbed in our childish plays and games with the maternal cousins in *Nanihaal* that despite being the most gifted child or student of my school back at my village, there was a lot happening in the backyard of Providence to subvert all this seemingly well-settled scenario for me and my mother. In the wake of his all apparent complicity in the beating of the PT teacher at the town school by the rowdy students, my father had been eased off from the school –

otherwise, too, he was merely an *ad hoc* teacher, not a permanent one, the fact which, being a duffer, he never could realise; and could never mend his ways to compensate for his vulnerable and fickle status at school. Instead, he depended too much on the bygone glory and clout of his rowdy relatives like *Bhaiyaajee* and *Pardhaan Chaachaa,* instead of improving his skills and attainments so as to justify his entitlement to the post of employment. This was a fallout of feudalism. So he had lost his job at school at this juncture unbeknown to us, nay, to me, the little kid.

XXX

Table of Contents

The End

English Books by *'Videh'*

Hypocrisy & Reality (fiction series: 9 books)

'Hypocrisy & Reality' is a fiction series comprising multiple books – novels. The fiction is aimed at depicting the hypocrisy of human society in every respect, be it the upbringing and treatment of babies, toddlers, children, adolescents, youths, or be it the treatment meted out to adults, aged ones, those who are closely related with oneself, with one's blood; not to speak of those called strangers or outsiders. Barring a rarity, nobody cares two hoots for the sentiments or security and safety of other living creatures on this sole planet nurturing 'living' beings!

Book 1: Beyond the Pale (fiction)

'Beyond the Pale' of Time & Space is the first volume of the long fiction series 'Hypocrisy & Reality' and as the name suggests, it deals with the timespan in the life of the protagonist when one had not even had a tryst with the concepts of Time and Space, nor did they make any difference in one's life if those ubiquitous phenomena were not taken cognizance of. Those were the years before the realm of schooling, the arena of perfect unconcern for the written letters, words, or numbers.

Book 2: Wilderness of Literacy (fiction)

'Wilderness of Literacy' is the second volume in the long fiction series 'Hypocrisy & Reality' and, as the name suggests, it takes the protagonist in the arena of letters, words, and numbers: the realm of what we call the 'literacy'. The experience of a child while treading this seemingly dreaded as well as untrodden landscape is nothing short of venturing into a wilderness; of course, led and mentored first by one's parents and thereafter invariably by their preceptors -- the masters -- all of whom have a tremendous amount of impact on the future human being that emerges from their inputs given and endeavours made towards making a man, the humanity.

Book 3: Advent of Time (fiction)

'Advent of Time' is the third volume in the long fiction series entitled 'Hypocrisy & Reality' and covers the schooling period when the protagonist discovered the phenomenon of Time, and also, figuratively he felt that it was then his time, even as, he mysteriously discovered his latent potential and wisdom catapulting himself into the uppermost orbits of glory, fame and all round applause from his classmates, masters as well as teachers. To his own amazement as well as bewilderment! Nevertheless, this providential blessing was not without its blemishes in the shape of rancour and envy of fellow classmates and their patrons towards him. Even as, Nature never allows anybody pleasure and praise without at the same time associating with them the equivalent amount of pain and back-biting!

Book 4: Devoid of Shelter (fiction)

'Devoid of Shelter', the fourth volume in the long fiction series 'Hypocrisy & Reality' furthers the journey of the protagonist into the world where he discovered to his dismay that he had no place on the globe which he could call as his home; he had no place of his own where he could take shelter during the day, and during the night. He somehow made do with seeking shelter with the relatives – maternal chiefly; not as a transitory phenomenon, but for good, until he himself took command of his life, snatching himself away from the indolent lifestyle of his parents. He also discovered during the refuge that however meritorious one might be, without the good base of ancestry, one was not considered as such.

Book 5: Price of Refuge (fiction)

'Price of Refuge', the fifth volume in the fiction series 'Hypocrisy & Reality' furthers the journey of the protagonist into the world when he returned to his paternal relatives and found to his dismay that his father was absolutely incapable of arranging a dwelling of his own. Also, he found himself to be a mute subject to child abuse at the hands of none other than supposedly an elder cousin of his, the son of his so-called benefactors who provided refuge in their vacant house. That was the price paid by the child for the indolence and handicaps of an unworthy father for seeking shelter under the tutelage of so-called relatives. No refuge seemingly looking innocuous goes without some price to be paid either by self, spouse or one's children.

Book 6: Hatred towards Love (fiction)

'Hatred towards Love', the sixth volume in the fiction series 'Hypocrisy & Reality' furthers the journey of the protagonist into the world where to his amusement he found himself catapulted into the realm of a celebrity or at least a child prodigy as far as the small rural catchment area was concerned. By virtue of his giftedness in the realm of studies and his bewitching countenance, the classmates, especially, the lasses of her age could not help restraining themselves from loving him; and they did it overtly, without caring for the opinions and feelings of other class-fellows. Albeit the protagonist himself wallowed in the faulty ideology that having any truck with fair sex was anathema and a great sin which could not be washed away in later life.

Book 7: Towards the Yoga (fiction)

'Towards the Yoga', the seventh volume in the fiction series 'Hypocrisy & Reality' dwells on the period in the journey of life of the protagonist when he was at the pinnacle of his bodily prowess and psychic acuity, thanks to his habit of pursuing *Yogaasans* regularly as well as religiously. As though something divine was associated with the pursuit of *Yogaasans*, his father luckily could get an *ad hoc* teacher's job in the town school too; however, that was not to be sustained throughout for at the fag-end of the academic session, his father fell out with the Principal of school and was expelled. *Yoga,* nevertheless, gave the protagonist a hue that was unparallelled, and which materialised into the worldly as well as societal fame for him.

Book 8: On the Descent (fiction)

'On the Descent', the eighth volume in the fiction series 'Hypocrisy & Reality' takes the protagonist over the hump. He was then a ward of such a guardian who did not have any wherewithal to run his household, yet had no qualms about begetting more issues, more and more at that. Agriculture, of course, he had as an inheritance but he was by nature averse to anything even distantly associated with agriculture or Nature, for that matter. Any industrious as well as expedient agriculturalist would have eked out one's livelihood quite easily from the fifteen *beeghaa*s of arable land his father had inherited from his resourceful, brave as well as powerful ancestors, but not he.

Book 9: In the Exile (fiction)

'In the Exile', the ninth volume in the fiction series 'Hypocrisy & Reality' furthers the journey of the protagonist into the world where post his dramatic jump into the orbit of fame in the wake of his High School result, he found himself entirely in a barren land where he could see no ray of hope from his father, even as, the latter was totally incapable of arranging the means to further the studies for his exceptionally gifted son. For the first time, the protagonist realised that his father was incapable of meeting his requirements for pursuing further studies. He was already suffering emotionally having been separated from his mother for the first time! This was for him like an exile, that too, very uncomfortable!

Bewailing Muse (poetry)

Be it the sage *Valmeeki* or be it the modern poet *Sumitraa Nandan Pant*, both have held that poetry has its founts in heart and is the outcome of extreme sorrow, misery or pangs of separation. Poetry cannot be created; it gets engendered out of compulsion. From the heart! Heart's language is poetry or musing! I have offered to christen them as Muse: 'Bewailing Muse'; the first musings out of wailings! Nevertheless, I am tempted not to treat them as children's literature for I sense some

substantial element, too, in them. The period of the composition of these poems is from 1972 to 1976; and I feel that my wailings have not fallen on deaf ears, so to say, given my present circumstances of life which are totally opposite to the then prevailing ones!

Chambellion (drama: comedietta)

In the genre of Drama (Comedietta), here is the playlet *'Chambellion'* that exposes the bizarre reality of the political developments post transfer of reins from the whites to the yellow people in the guise of 'Democracy' and 'Independence'; whereas actually the latter have been pursuing their dynastic agenda and propagating their own family fiefdoms that have flourished like weeds in multitudes in the void created by annihilation of Princely states and Landlords. Allegorically, it may be compared with the weed flourishing in an agricultural field which has remained unsown after harvest of the previous crop. For the subjects, verily, there is no Freedom whatsoever, in literal sense.

Brainy Beasts (short stories)

This is an anthology of short stories, included wherein are four short stories or farces, so to say, that is, anecdotes including the 'In An Illegible Script', which is the English version of the author's *Hindee* short story *'Anpadh Lipi Mein...* (अनपढ़ लिपि में)*'* that was first published in now extinct though the then prestigious *Hindee* magazine the 'Kaadambinee' way back in July, 1992, with quite an applause and accolades from the sides of kind readers! Other stories or anecdotes are also those published in other places, i.e. journals of variegated hues. Nothing uttered in these works is meaningless; this conviction is at work behind the inspiration to publish them in book form for kind readers.

Search for Life (translation of 'Hatyaaree Sadee Mein Jeevan Kee Khoj' (हत्यारी सदी में जीवन की खोज))

English Translation by *'Videh' Arvind Kumar* of *Hindee* poetry book *'Hatyaaree Sadee Mein Jeevan Kee Khoj'* (हत्यारी सदी में जीवन की खोज) by renowned young poet *'Nirvikaar' Mukesh Kumar*. This book has earned *'Nirvikaar'* the award of *'Jai Shankar Prasaad Puraskaar'* of Rs. One Lac from the *'Rajya Karmchaaree Saahitya Sansthaan, Uttar Pradesh'*. On the *Hindee* book *'Hatyaaree Sadee Mein Jeevan Kee Khoj,'* critiques by renowned personalities -- both young and old -- like *Ashwaghosh, Prempaal Sharmaa, Rajeev Saxena, Dr Anoop Singh, Dr Devkee Nandan Sharmaa, Manoj Kumaar Jhaa, Gautam Rajarshi,* etc have been published in various journals and magazines. The renowned critic Dr *Om Nishchal* has included this anthology in the select category for *'Kavya Paridrishya'* of 2017 amongst the famous poetry books.

Reality of Invisible (translation of 'Adrishya Kaa Yathaarth' (अदृश्य का यथार्थ))

English translation by *'Videh' Arvind Kumar* of the *Hindee* poetry book *'Adrishya Kaa Yathaarth'* (अदृश्य का यथार्थ) by renowned poet *'Ashwaghosh' Om Prakaash Sharmaa. 'Ashwaghosh'* -- a well-known moniker of *Hindee*

world! A litterateur of impeccable renown! Praised by multitudes -- both in literary and plebeian spheres! He has been composing prolifically -- having published over two dozen books spanning all the genre! The thesis, the short stories, the short epics, the anthologies, the new genre songs, the *ghazals*, the poetry for children *et al.* Covering all age groups! He has been honoured with many awards in literary and academic fields by prestigious institutions.

Nagasaki: Bomb & Aftermath (commentary on the first novel of Nobel Laureate, Kazuo Ishiguro) (Displayed on Oxford bookstore)

This is a work of literary study into the first novel 'The Pale View of Hills' by 2017 Literature Nobel Laureate, Kazuo Ishiguro, who has narrated in a mesmerising style of story telling the tale of Japanese society undergoing change in the aftermath of dropping of atomic bomb. The Americans not only vanquished and occupied the Japanese military and land by dropping the most lethal weapon never before heard of – the atomic bomb – on two of the Japanese cities, one of which was Nagasaki which witnessed this technological devastation on 8th of August, 1945, but also, occupied the minds and hearts of Japanese youth, both men and women. The youth of Japan started decrying everything old and conventional including their erstwhile education system and the ideologies of patriotism and nationalism.

Procreation, the Adorable (English summary of Shiv Puraan)

The *Shiva-ling* has ever been a matter of amazement and mystery for mankind. That something obscure is there behind the adoration of such a carnal symbol as *ling* irrespective of the same being that of a deity called *Shiva* has ever been lingering in my mind. Why should a large majority of population in this land – from north to south -- worship the genitals so openly, so brazenly? So reverently! *Shiva* is supposed to be a mythological persona, in existence too long back in time, who might have been the pioneer in realizing the spectacular qualities of *ling* and *yoni,* specifically, those of converting the *sthaavar* (the insensate) into *jangam* (the sensate) and those of creating the *satva-lok,* (conscious beings).

Self-Styled Sovereign, the Judiciary (Dramatic deliberation on the state of judiciary)

This is in fact an academic deliberation on the functioning and reality of the judicial system prevalent in India post what they euphemistically call the 'Independence' or, literally, the *'Aazaadee'*. Whose Independence was it anyway? For whom? Except for the ruling class? The lawyers first, and then the hooligans of *Chambal*. Nonetheless, the judiciary of the free country turned out to be one step further than its new crop of leaders; they usurped the entire authority from the latter in subtle moves one after the other. In olden epochs, the autocratic *Sultaans* or *Baadshaahs* dispensed justice purely depending upon their whims and fancies, which were incidental to the moods and tantrums of the Sovereign. Historically as well, the Real Sovereign was the one who dispensed justice. The Judiciary in Indian Republic soon realised this and acted.

XXX

'विदेह' रचित हिंदी ग्रंथ

अनपढ़ लिपि (कहानी-संग्रह)

'विदेह' अरविन्द कुमार की आठ हिंदी कहानियों का संकलन! संकलन की पहली कहानी 'अनपढ लिपि में ...' जुलाई, 1992 में प्रतिष्ठित हिंदी पत्रिका 'कादंबिनी' में छपी थी। 'सिग्नेचर' भी स्वच्छता के प्रति सरकारी महकमे की विद्रूपात्मक मनोदशा का कड़वा चित्रण है। 'ताकि आप अपने पक्ष में रहें!' नये प्रकार के कर्मचारियों की मानसिकता को इंगित करती है। फिर फिर वही लोग' भेड़-बकरियों की तरह दुरुपयोग किये जा रहे जन-समुदाय के विषय में कहानी है। 'अपार्थाइड' : वस्तुतः तो, शक्तिशाली और निर्बल का भेद ही असली रंग-भेद है। 'नया वेद' 'आज़ादी' नाम से वही पारम्परिक पद्धति चतुराई-पूर्वक 'नया संविधान' के नाम से चलाये जाने की पोल-पट्टी खोलती है। 'पहली कमाई' कहानी का आख्यान कल्पना से भी अधिक विस्मयकारी है! 'भगवान को पैसा' समाज और सरकार दोनों ही की धन के प्रति जो दृष्टि है, उस पर तीखा व्यंग्य है।

पाषाण-युग (कहानी-संग्रह)

'विदेह' अरविन्द कुमार की सात हिंदी कहानियों का संकलन! संकलन की पहली कहानी 'ब्लॉक का पेड़' आज के समाज में क्षीण होते हुए आपसी सौहार्द्र, एवं अजनबियों के प्रति बढ़ते अकारण वैमनस्य, को बिंबित करती हुई सच्चाई है। मेरी

ज्ञाति' भारत में जातियों के हास्यास्पद 'प्रहसन' – फ़ार्स (farce) -- को चित्रित करके इसकी विद्रूपता को व्यंजित करती है। हिंदू-मुसलमान' साम्प्रदायिकता के प्रश्न को व्यक्तियों – दो घनिष्ठ मित्रों -- के स्तर पर परीक्षण करके देखती है। 'मुर्गबाज' समय की नब्ज पर हाथ रखने की कोशिश है। मंदिरों, मस्जिदों, गुरुद्वारों, गिरजाघरों में ...' साम्प्रदायिक कट्टरता की निर्थकता को व्यंजित करने के लिए है, जो मृत्यु के पर्दे के पीछे कितनी हास्यास्पद बन जाती है! ऐ अधर्मी!' आदमी की नस्ल को बदलने की नाहक कोशिश कही जा सकती है। 'राक्षस' इस नये शासन-प्रशासन में व्याप्त भ्रष्टाचार पर एक व्यंग्यात्मक टिप्पणी है, और बताती है कि राक्षस कोई कपोल-कल्पना नहीं है, बल्कि आज भी एक वास्तविकता है।

निसर्ग (कहानी-संग्रह)

'विदेह' अरविन्द कुमार की सात हिंदी कहानियों का संकलन! संकलन की पहली कहानी 'मुलाक़ात एक बड़े लेखक से' एक बड़े लेखक और एक आम आदमी के जीवन के साम्य और अंतर दोनों को ही उजागर करती है। 'फाड़ी हुई कविता' एक ऐसे पति की व्यथा-कथा है, जो एक कवि एवं साहित्यकार भी है। 'नया साल' में कुछ भी नया नहीं होता, फिर भी सारी दुनिया किस कदर बाबली हुई रहती है। 'हितैषिणी' शादी जैसी संस्थाओं के पाखण्ड, फ़रेब एवं परम्पराओं से चिपकाव की विद्रूपता पर सशक्त प्रहार करती है। 'छोटे-से शरीर में क़ैदी' शिशुमन की विवशता को चित्रित करती है; वह पूरी तरह माँ-बाप की मूर्खताओं पर निर्भर रहने को विवश है। 'निसर्ग' एक रोमांटिक कहानी है। 'टूट-टूटकर गिरते सितारे' दिखाती है कि कैसे समाज अपने ही शिकंजे में फँसा रहकर ही परेशान होता रहता है!

आर्त-गान (कविता-संग्रह)

'वियोगी होगा पहला कवि, आह से उपजा होगा गान

उमड़कर आँखों से चुपचाप, बही होगी कविता अनजान!'

(सुमित्रा नंदन पंत)

या

'मा निषाद त्वम् गम: प्रतिष्ठाम् शाश्वती समा:

यत् क्रौंच मिथुनादेकम् त्वम् वधी: काम मोहितम्!'

(महर्षि वाल्मीकि)

चाहे तो आदि कवि वाल्मीकि हों, चाहे फिर छायावादी कवि पंत हों, एक बात तो तय है, कि कविता वियोग या विषाद या शोक से उत्सृजित होती है। पहले-पहल की रचनाएँ हैं ये – जीवन के पहले-प्रहर की; अतः बच्चों के उपयुक्त ही हो सकती हैं। बाल-कविता! बाल-कविता इसे मैंने फिर भी इसलिए नहीं कहा है, क्योंकि इनमें मुझे कुछ सार भी सन्निहित लगता रहा है; एकदम तो बकवास नहीं ही हैं ये, जैसी कि बाल (अबोध) - कविता की प्रकृति और प्रवृत्ति होती है। ये कविताएँ 1972 से 1976 के काल-खंड में सृजित हैं; और अभी लगभग अर्ध-शती की परिपक्व दृष्टि से भी परिमार्जित!

काल-क्रंदन (कविता-संग्रह)

जीवन के प्रथम प्रहर की हृदयाभिव्यक्तियों (1972 से 1976 तक) के 'आर्त-गान' के बाद, 1979 से 1990 तक के द्वादश वर्षीय काल-खण्ड में मैंने जो क्रंदन किया था, उसे मैंने कविता कहा; और उन कविताओं का 'काल-रेख' नाम मैंने चुना था; क्योंकि काल की छाती पर 12 वर्षों तक मैं जो घिसटता रहा था, उस लकीर पीटने को 'काल-रेख' कहना ही मुझे रुच रहा था। परन्तु, कुछ काव्यात्मक स्फुरणा के वश, कुछ काल-अंतराल के प्रभाव-वश मैं अब इसे 'काल-क्रंदन' ही कहना अधिक समीचीन समझ रहा हूँ। साहित्य -- और इसीलिए कविता भी -- जीवन के मूल की अर्थात् सत्य की खोज है: सत्य की परख, यथार्थ की परख! इसमें सब कुछ सुनने-सुनाने, गाने-गवाने ही योग्य है, ऐसा दावा मैं नहीं करता। परन्तु, क्या पढ़ने-पढ़ाने योग्य है, और क्या नहीं, इसका निर्णय भी तो मैं नहीं कर सकता; क्योंकि इसका कण-कण मेरा नितांत निजी सच है! इसमें कितना किस और किसी का भी सच प्रस्तुत है, यह निर्णय उन्हीं पर!

अननुभूत काल (कविता-संग्रह)

अब यह तीसरी काव्य-पुस्तक है! एकदम नवीन काल से सम्बंधित! अभी-अभी हो गुज़रे बड़े मानवीय हादसे को रेखांकित करती हुई: कोरोना की महा-आपदा! विश्व-आपदा! जो न कभी हुई

थी, और आशा एवम् प्रार्थना ही कर सकते हैं, न कभी भविष्य में होगी! एकदम नये रूप में दुनिया को सोचने को मजबूर होना पड़ा: 'ऐसा भी हो सकता है?' बेतहाशा भागम-भाग में लगी दुनिया अचानक रुक-सी गयी; नहीं, रुक ही गयी – शब्दशः। वायुयान रुक गये, रेलयान रुक गये, बसें रुक गयीं, सारे वाहन रुक गये। मंदिर, मश्जिद, गुरुद्वारे और चर्च भी बंद हो गये: परमात्मा के घर थे वे! हैं! मक्का, मदीना बंद हो गये। वेटिकन बंद हो गया। वह चिरंतन अटूट आस्था जो रुकने का नाम नहीं लेती थी, और आए-दिन छोटी-छोटी बातों पर सिर-फुटव्वल को बेताब रहती थी, अचानक अपने को सकपकाता हुआ पाने लगी। क्या वह बस आस्था ही भर थी, दुनियावी प्राणियों को भरमाने के लिए; क्या उसमें कोई पारमार्थिक सार न था? तार्किक मन यह सोचने को विवश हो गया। इस कोरोना-काल ने बहुत सारे पाखण्ड-मण्डन किये हैं!

अम्बेडकर-स्मृति (नाटिका)

जाति की समस्या भारत देश के लिए भयंकर होती जा रही है। यह जाति ही है जिसके चलते भारत-भूमि आक्रांताओं के समक्ष प्रणत हो गयी थी। कड़वी सच्चाई यह है कि राजनीतिक चतुराई के चलते 'सत्ताधीशों' ने अपने आप को 'ऊँचा' और सत्ता से 'वंचित' जनों को 'नीचा' मानना शुरू कर दिया। 'आज़ादी' के अधकचरे प्रयोग के चलते स्थिति और भी भयावह हो गयी है; 'नीचे लोग' ऊँचे लोगों को गरियाते रहते हैं: उसके लिए वे 'मनु-स्मृति' नाम की किसी पौराणिक पुस्तक को गरियाते रहते हैं, जबकि वास्तविकता यह है कि आधुनिक भारत के 99.99 प्रतिशत लोगों ने उस पुस्तक का पढ़ना तो दूर, नाम तक नहीं सुना है। उधर, नये सत्ताधीशों ने नयी स्मृति लिखकर -- संविधान लिखकर (जिसकी ड्राफ्टिंग समिति के अध्यक्ष होने के नाते अम्बेडकर को श्रेय मिला हुआ है) – पूर्ववर्ती समाज-व्यवस्था एवं अर्थ-व्यवस्था को एक सिरे से नकार और नेस्तनाबूद कर दिया है। समाज के बीच इस पर जो बहस चल रही है, उसी का एक छोटा सा नमूना है यह एकांकी!

प्रिय-प्रवास (संकलन, 'हरिऔध' के महाकाव्य का)

'प्रिय-प्रवास' हिंदी -- खड़ी बोली -- का प्रथम महाकाव्य है, जो स्वनाम धन्य महाकवि अयोध्या सिंह उपाध्याय 'हरिऔध' की अमर कृति है। अत्यंत सुमधुर काव्य के रूप में युग-पुरुष श्रीकृष्ण के गोकुल से मथुरा प्रवास और उनके वियोग से व्यथित गोकुल-वासियों की विरह-वेदना का सरस चित्रण इसमें है। वह एक प्रकार से हर प्राणी की वेदना ही है, जो वह उस समय अनुभव करता है जब कोई स्वजन प्रवास हेतु जाता है या प्रयाण करता है, जो कि संसृति का अपरिहार्य लक्षण ही है। आसक्ति, मोह और ममता सब दुःखों का मूल है; जबकि ज्ञान दुःखों से मुक्ति का साधन! इस महा-आख्यान का यही सार अथच् केंद्रीय संदेश समझ में आता है! 'प्रिय-प्रवास' विरह, बिछुड़ने की वेदना, नैसर्गिक प्रेम और विश्व-कल्याण के संदेश का ही महाकाव्यात्मक सरस रूप है। 'विदेह' अरविन्द कुमार ने इस अद्भुत साहित्यिक कृति को पुनर्संकलित एवं पुनर्मुद्रित करके इसकी एक संक्षिप्त गद्य-कथा भी इसमें प्रस्तुत की है।

प्रार्थना एवं प्राणांश (संकलित प्रेरक काव्यांश)

बहुत ही सरस और सार्थक प्रार्थनाओं एवं प्रेरणादायी काव्यांशों का संचयन है यह! जो न जाने कहाँ-कहाँ से 'विदेह' अरविंद कुमार ने अपनी रुचि अनुकूल संकलित एवं सम्पादित किया है, उन सभी मनीषियों के प्रति हार्दिक आभार व्यक्त करते हुए, जिनकी रचनाएँ और रचनाओं के प्राणांश इसमें संकलित किये गये हैं। जीवन, मृत्यु के वाहन के आगमन की प्रतीक्षा में रत यात्री के कार्य-कलाप और मनोदशा के अतिरिक्त और क्या है! इस प्रतीक्षा में क्या-क्या अनहोनी अनुभूतियाँ नहीं होतीं! इस प्रतीक्षा को कम कष्टकर करने के लिए काव्य-शास्त्र अनुश्रवण की अनुशंसा मनीषियों ने की है। साथ ही, प्रार्थना के माहात्म्य को भी स्वीकारा है।

मनो पुब्बंगमा धम्मा, मनो सेट्ठा मनोमया!'

भगवान बुद्ध ने मन से ही सृजित होता हुआ इस सकल प्रपञ्च को बताया है। अत: मन को शुचि एवं निष्कंप रखकर आप संसार का अनुभव बदल सकते हैं। जब सभी कुछ कल्पित है, तो सबको अपना मत अनुभव जैसा ही लगता है। परन्तु, है वस्तुतः सब कुछ कपोल-कल्पित ही: न इसे सत्य कहने का कोई तात्पर्य है, न असत्य कहने का! बस मन को साधने का साधनभर है प्रार्थना!

महामुनि वाल्मीकि रचित् इतिहास :
उत्तरकाण्ड (वाल्मीकि के उत्तरकाण्ड का गद्यांतरित सारांश)

'रामायण' आदिकाव्य है, न केवल भारतवर्ष का, अपितु सकल मानव-समाज का भी। महर्षि वाल्मीकि-कृत यह काव्य-पुस्तक वस्तुतः तत्कालीन इतिहास है: उस राजवंश का, जिसकी कीर्ति हज़ारों वर्ष पश्चात् भी आज तक अक्षुण्ण है। उस राजवंश के तत्कालीन यशस्वी सम्राट 'राम' का इसमें वर्णन है। राम-राज्य की व्यवस्था, जिसका वर्णन ऋषि ने किया है, आज भी शासन-व्यवस्था के हेतु आदर्श मानी जाती है।

लेखक ने संस्कृत के ग्रंथ का मात्र सार रूप यहाँ प्रस्तुत किया है; सब प्रकार की काव्यात्मकता और अतिशयोक्तियों का निवारण करते हुए। साथ ही, आलंकारिकता को आधुनिक संदर्भों से जोड़ते हुए ऐतिहासिक-वैज्ञानिक अर्थों में भी विषय को समझाने का प्रयास किया है।

कितना यह किसको भाता है, यह तो हर व्यक्ति की अपनी-अपनी रुचि और सोच पर निर्भर करेगा; बहरहाल, लेखक ने अपना दृष्टिकोण प्रस्तुत किया है, वह भी इस चिन्ता से कि नयी पीढ़ी अपनी बहुमूल्य विरासत – गौरवशाली इतिहास -- की ओर एकदम ध्यान नहीं दे रही है। उसका एक कारण ग्रंथों का संस्कृत में होना, और दूसरा अत्यधिक प्रतीकात्मक होने के कारण कपोल-कल्पित-सा लगना, भी हो सकता है; उसी कारण का निवारण करने का यह विनीत प्रयास है।

XXX

लेखक-परिचय

'विदेह' अरविन्द कुमार

भारतीय साहित्य की उदात्त पीठिका को आधुनिक संदर्भों से संपृक्त करने वाले सारस्वत साधक एवं विशिष्ट लेखन-शैली के प्रणेता वरिष्ठ साहित्यकार श्री अरविन्द कुमार 'विदेह' का जन्म 6 अप्रैल 1957 ई को उत्तर प्रदेश के गौतमबुद्धनगर जनपद की जेवर तहसील के छोटे-से गाँव 'मारहरा' में हुआ था। आपके माता-पिता की मानव-मूल्यों में गहरी आस्था रही है। सीमित संसाधनों, बल्कि विपन्नता, के बावज़ूद भी आप सफलता के लाभी हुए। आपने तत्कालीन आगरा विश्वविद्यालय के अलीगढ़ स्थित धर्मसमाज कॉलेज से भौतिक विज्ञान में स्नातकोत्तर उपाधि प्राप्त की है। आप देश के प्रतिष्ठित बैंक – भारतीय स्टेट बैंक – में दीर्घकालीन सेवा प्रदान करने के उपरांत दिसम्बर, 2018 में सहायक महाप्रबंधक के पद से सेवा निवृत्त हुए हैं।

श्री 'विदेह' छात्र-जीवन से ही अत्यंत मेधावी रहे हैं। विज्ञान-संवर्ग के विद्यार्थी होते हुए भी आपकी साहित्य के प्रति गहरी अभिरुचि रही है। साहित्य के प्रति आपका अनुराग इतना प्रबल रहा है कि बैंकिंग सेक्टर में अति व्यस्त जीवन-शैली वाली नौकरी करते हुए भी आप साहित्य और लेखन से अनवरत रूप से जुड़े रहे हैं। उनकी रचनाएँ तत्कालीन 'कादम्बिनी' जैसी लब्ध-प्रतिष्ठ पत्रिकाओं में काफ़ी पहले छप चुकी हैं; और उनके अन्य लेख एवं कविताएँ अन्य हिंदी, अंग्रेज़ी पत्र-पत्रिकाओं में यदा-कदा छपते रहे हैं। साथ ही, आपने हिंदी एवं अंग्रेजी भाषा के साहित्य का विशद अध्ययन एवं सृजन किया है। संस्कृत एवं पाली भाषा के साहित्य में भी आपकी गहरी अभिरुचि है।

विभिन्न विधाओं में आपने अब तक 27 ग्रंथों का प्रणयन किया है, जिनमें 17 अंग्रेजी एवं 10 हिंदी भाषा में हैं। हिंदी की पुस्तकों में 03 कहानी-संग्रह (अनपढ़ लिपि, पाषाण युग, निसर्ग); 03 कविता-संग्रह (आर्त-गान, काल-क्रन्दन, अननुभूत काल); 01 नाटिका (अम्बेडकर-स्मृति); 01 काव्य-संचयन (प्रार्थना एवं प्राणांश) उल्लेखनीय हैं। इसके अतिरिक्त आपने खड़ी बोली के प्रथम महाकाव्य 'प्रिय-प्रवास' को भी पुनर्संकलित एवं पुनर्मुद्रित किया है; तथा साथ ही,

112

वाल्मीकि रामायण के उत्तरकाण्ड का गद्यांतरण इतिहास के दृष्टिकोण से आपने 'महामुनि वाल्मीकि रचित् इतिहास: रामायण – उत्तरकाण्ड' नामक पुस्तक के रूप में किया है।

अंग्रेजी भाषा में आपकी उपन्यास श्रृंखला 'Hypocrisy & Reality' है जिसके अब तक 9 खण्ड वह प्रस्तुत कर चुके हैं (Beyond the Pale; Wilderness of Literacy; Advent of Time; Devoid of Shelter; Price of Refuge; Hatred towards Love; Towards the *Yoga*; On the Descent; In the Exile)। इसके अतिरिक्त, 01 Comedietta (*Chambellion*); 01 Short Story collection (Brainy Beasts); 01 Poetry anthology (Bewailing Muse); 01 Drama (Self-styled Sovereign, the Judiciary); पौराणिक ग्रंथ 'शिव-पुराण' के आधुनिक संदर्भों में अध्ययन पर आधारित 01 पुस्तक (Procreation, the Adorable); 2017 के साहित्य नोबेल पुरस्कार विजेता, Kazuo Ishiguro, के प्रथम उपन्यास 'A Pale View of the Hills' पर आधारित 01 समीक्षात्मक ग्रंथ (Nagasaki: Bomb & Aftermath) हैं।

'विदेह' जितने मौलिक सर्जक हैं उतने ही समर्थ अनुवादक भी हैं। उन्होंने हिंदी के 02 काव्य-संग्रहों – 'निर्विकार' मुकेश के 'हत्यारी सदी में जीवन की खोज', और 'अश्वघोष' ओमप्रकाश शर्मा के 'अदृश्य का यथार्थ' – का काव्यात्मक अनुवाद अंग्रेजी में किया है, जो क्रमश: 'Search for Life' एवं 'Reality of Invisible' के नाम से प्रकाशित हुई हैं।

'विदेह' के व्यक्तित्व का निर्माण घोर विपन्नता और कठोर संघर्षों ने किया है, जिसका प्रभाव उनकी लेखन-शैली पर निर्भीक अभिव्यक्ति और बेवाकी के रूप में देखा जा सकता है। आपके जीवन का अनुभव अत्यन्त व्यापक रहा है। आपने विपन्नता भी भोगी है, और सुख-सुविधा-सम्पन्न अमेरिकी जीवन भी जीया है; साथ ही, अनेक विदेश-यात्राओं का भी आपको अनुभव है।

केवल साहित्य ही नहीं, 'विदेह' की प्रवृत्तियों में ध्यान-साधना, विपश्यना, योग-साधना, प्राकृतिक-जीवन, आरोग्य, शाकाहार, बागवानी, पर्यटन और पैदल भ्रमण भी सम्मिलित हैं।

2024 के हिंदी दिवस पर – 14 सितंबर को – 'विदेह' को 'शुभम् साहित्य, कला एवम् संस्कृति संस्थान' द्वारा उनके सर्वोच्च सम्मान 'शुभम् रत्न' से सम्मानित किया गया।

'विदेह' की पुस्तकें 'Notion Press', Blue Rose One, Amazon और Flipkart पर तीनों ही प्रारूपों – ebooks, paperback एवम् hard cover – में उपलब्ध हैं।

XXX

About the Author

'Videh' Arvind Kumar

An unflinching adorer of the goddess of wisdom, the *Saraswatee*, and the one who has associated the lofty traditions of Indian literature with the present day contexts, and also, an author of an uncanny style of his own, the seasoned litterateur, *'Videh' Arvind Kumar,* was born on 6th of April, 1957, at a hamlet called *'Maar-Haraa'* in *Jewar Tehseel* of *Gautam Buddha Nagar* distt. in UP. His parents were staunch votaries of human values. Despite unbearable financial constraints, rather extreme wretchedness, he overcame the hurdles of existence and succeeded. He is a post-graduate in Physics from D S College, *Aleegarh,* affiliated to the then *Aagaraa* University. He retired as an Asstt General Manager from the esteemed Bank – State Bank of India – after putting in a long as well as illustrious service there.

'Videh' has been meritorious ever since his school days. Despite being a science stream scholar, he has been showing a keen interest in literature all along. His bonding with literature has been so strong that notwithstanding his pursuing such a busy job as Banking, he managed to sustain his love for literature. His works have been published decades back in the then esteemed magazines such as 'Kaadambinee'. Also, his stray articles and compositions have found place in various magazines and journals now and then. Besides, he has been a voracious reader of literature and other stuff both in *Hindee* and English languages, apart from himself being a prolific writer and a poet. He is also an adorer of the literature in *Sanskrit* and *Pali* languages.

In variegated genre he has composed as many as 27 books so far, of which, 17 are in English and 10 in *Hindee*. Among the *Hindee* books, there are 03 story anthologies (*Anapadh Lipi; Paashaan Yug; Nisarg*); 03 poetry anthologies (*Aaart Gaan; Kaal Krandan; Ananubhoot Kaal*); 01 drama (*Ambedkar Smriti*); 01 collection of select poetic pieces (*Praarthanaa evam Praanaansh)*. Aside of this, he has compiled, commented, edited and got re-published the first epic of the *Khadee Bolee Hindee*, the *Priya Pravaas*; and a book entitled *'Mahaamuni Vaalmeeki Rachit Itihaas: Raamaayan -- Uttar Kaand'* which presents, in succinct prose form, the ancient history of India as narrated in the most ancient epic.

As regards English oeuvre of *'Videh'*, he has so far published 9 volumes of the long fiction series 'Hypocrisy & Reality' (Beyond the Pale; Wilderness of Literacy; Advent of Time; Devoid of Shelter; Price of Refuge; Hatred towards Love; Towards the *Yoga*; On the Descent; In the Exile) with yet more planned to come. Besides, 01 Comedietta (*Chambellion*); 01 Short Story collection (Brainy Beasts); 01 Poetry anthology (Bewailing Muse); 01 Drama (Self-Styled Sovereign, the Judiciary); 01 book based on the study of mythological volume *'Shiva Puraan'* in the present day context (Procreation, the Adorable); 01 commentary book on the first novel – 'A Pale View of the Hills' -- of the 2017 Nobel Literature laureate, Kazuo Ishiguro (Nagasaki: Bomb & Aftermath) are other books.

Not only an original writer as well as thinker, but also, a capable and versatile translator is *'Videh'* inasmuch as he has translated in English free verse form 02 *Hindee* poetry anthologies, viz. *'Hatyaaree Sadee Mein Jeevan Kee Khoj'* of *'Nirvikaar'* Mukesh Kumaar, and *'Adrishya Kaa Yathaarth'* of *'Ashwaghosh'* Omprakaash Sharmaa with the titles of the books being *seriatim* as 'Search for Life' and 'Reality of Invisible'.

The persona of *'Videh'* has been moulded by constant struggles and abject adversities, which have metamorphosed into his style of narration being quite frank as well as bland, if only straightforward.

His experiences of life are multifarious. He has not only suffered the pangs of extreme poverty and adversity in his childhood, but also, enjoyed the comforts and pleasures of the modern world by living in America.

Besides, he has visited and toured in various foreign countries, too.

Not only in literature, but also, in exotic pursuits like meditation, spiritual practice, *Vipashyanaa, Yoga* practice, naturopathy, natural living, *Aarogya,* vegetarianism, gardening, tourism and long walks on foot *'Videh'* is equally active.

To add to his laurels, *'Videh'* has been honoured with their highest honour *'Shubham Ratna'* by the institution *'Shubham Saahitya, Kalaa Evam Sanskriti Sansthaan'* on the occasion of *Hindee Divas*, i.e. on 14th September, 2024.

The books of *'Videh'* are available in all the three formats, viz. eBooks, paperbacks and hardcovers from the Notion Press, Blue Rose One, Amazon and the Flipkart.

XXX

Table of Contents